Alone Inside the Night

Hello Again Series by Kat Halstead
Hello Again
Stranger in my Bed
Always You

Also by Kat Halstead
Secret Fantasy
Memories of Me and You
Silent Night
The Spirit Board
What Happened in Paris
Perfect Imperfections

Alone Inside the Night

Kat Halstead

Salty Rock Media

Halstead, Kat
Alone Inside the Night / Kat Halstead – 1st ed.
ISBN 9781079583489
1. Friends – Fiction.   2. Reunited Love – Fiction.   3. Vacation Romance – Fiction. I. Title: Alone Inside the Nights.

kathalstead.net
saltyrockmedia.com

For Lisa, Amy, Katie, and Holly
I wouldn't be writing still without
you gals and your support.
XOXO

CHAPTER 1

"She still hasn't asked you who your best man is going to be?" Iris pulled the cork out of the bottle of Pinot Noir before pouring it into the three glasses on her kitchen counter.

"Nope, do you think she knows deep down and is afraid for the confirmation?" Gage shrugged; he was getting married in less than a week. Tomorrow his friends Iris, James, Cordelia, and Duke would be going up to his parents' house in Coral Shore. It was all part of his grand plan before his wedding day.

James looked up from his phone, "So let me get this straight, you really think that Cordelia and Duke are just going to fall back in love when they see each other?"

"No, but I think being in Coral Shore for a few days before the wedding will be good for them. Hopefully, it will give them a chance to talk and clear the air. At the very least Duke can hopefully find out why she broke up with him." Gage took his glass of wine and sat down on the futon Iris had in the middle of her loft.

"Why force this, it's been almost eight years." Iris took her own wine glass and sat on the ottoman.

"Because, until they at the very least clear the air neither will really move on, I don't know about you but I'm tired of Noah Wilson still showing up as Cordelia's date to stuff."

"I can't stand that guy, he's so fake." James took a long sip of his wine before sitting very close to Iris.

"Okay, so if they clear the air, what happens next; Duke lives in Texas?" Iris picked up her phone scrolling through Twitter as they talked.

"That's up to them, but wouldn't it be better for all of us to have this in the past. Aren't you sick of not being able to tell Cordelia we're hanging out with Duke when he's in town? Don't you want for all of us to spend the same week at Coral Shore?"

"That would be nice." James's fingers traced lazy patterns on Iris's legs, Gage noticed, he always noticed.

"So, let's get this set into motion." Gage checked his phone, "Duke is going to arrive tomorrow morning, James you and he will be on the same train ride out with Iris and Cordelia. You've got to sit together."

"Yeah, that won't be awkward." Iris rolled her eyes as she leaned against James.

"They either fight or don't talk to each other."

"Or she falls into his lap." Iris giggled.

"Don't be obvious."

"Okay, okay." Iris took a sip of her wine, "We'll figure it out. Worst comes to worst we'll make them walk home from dinner tomorrow night."

"Oh, that's good." James smiled, "This might be fun."

"You don't get the neurotic one." Iris reminded him.

"Okay, if they fight, I'll deal with Cordelia; you can deal with Duke, deal?"

"Deal." They shook, which surprised Gage, he was sure he was going to witness a kiss between his two friends.

"I have a feeling that Cordelia and Duke are going to be reunited, that Corduke will be back together by the time I'm married."

"You know something, spill."

"When Duke was here for that trip in the spring, I found out something from Mr. Watson," Gage confessed.

"Wait, I think we're missing a few pieces of this story, Gage," James warned.

"Mr. Watson told me that every Christmas Eve he gets a call from the lady across the street from Cordelia's old room. Apparently, every year a blonde man climbs the fire escape. She calls Mr.

Watson to warn him of the strange man, and he always tells her not to worry, it's one of Cordelia's friends looking for the courage to talk to her."

"Watson helped you come up with this, didn't he?" Iris put her glass down on the floor.

"I can neither confirm nor deny if he is involved at all." His smile gave it away though.

"What else do you know Gage?" James looked at his friend, wondering what he knew that he didn't know.

"Everything I tell you in this room tonight is secret."

"Of course." They both agreed.

"Duke is moving back to New York; he rented that retail space in the Watson building."

"Wait the one that's got the brown paper up but is still empty even though Beverly took the for-rent sign down—wow Duke."

"Yeah, he's also rented the apartment that's available starting July first."

James's mouth dropped, "You are a wicked little man."

"This is going to be an interesting few days." Iris picked her glass up, "To the Corduke Reunion! Everyone should know the epic yet silly love story."

"Hashtag it, tweet it for prosperity." James joked, but the joke became a reality later that night after Iris had several more glasses of wine.

♥

@IrisLaArt
Let us tell you the story of 2 silly kids who were once in love but broke up, & we don't know why. #CordukeReunion @JamesSheath @GKNYC

@JamesSheath
You see once there was a boy named Duke, who moved from Texas to NYC. #CordukeReunion

@IrisLaArt
& there was a girl named Cordelia, who spent her whole life in the city when one day her bestie pushed her into the lap of a cowboy. #CordukeReunion

@JamesSheath
He was smitten, told his best friend back in Texas all about her, for hours on end. #CordukeReunion

@IrisLaArt
They could barely talk to each other at first until a fateful night at the library. #CordukeReunion

@GKNYC
Where they opened to each other & started to fall in love, well as much as possible when in the 7th grade. #CordukeReunion

@GKNYC
What they shared couldn't be denied, even when @IrisLaArt had a crush on the cowboy. #CordukeReunion

@IrisLaArt
Hey, we don't need to bring that up @GKNYC.

@GKNYC
Eventually, after a hiccup or 2, Cordelia & Duke started to date. #CordukeReunion

@JamesSheath
They dated all throughout high school. They were the sweet couple everyone loved & hated. #CordukeReunion

@JamesSheath
They got into different colleges though but agreed to stay together & do the long-distance thing. #CordukeReunion

@IrisLaArt
High school ended, but these 2 were so in love that Duke gave Cordelia a promise ring #CordukeReunion

@GKNYC
Then something happened, we don't know what even almost 8 years later. But Cordelia sent Duke the promise ring back. #CordukeReunion
@JamesSheath
She stopped talking to him, broke his heart. #CordukeReunion
@IrisLaArt
But he did something that broke hers first, we think. #CordukeReunion
@GKNYC
We really have no idea what happened #CordukeReunion but over the years we; their friends know one thing.
@GKNYC
We know that Cordelia and Duke are still crazy about each other, even though they haven't seen each other #CordukeReunion
@IrisLaArt
We kept waiting for them to run into each other, every spring break they went to the same location, the same week. #CordukeReunion
@JamesSheath
But they never saw each other, but tomorrow that all changes. #CordukeReunion
@GKNYC
Cordelia and Duke will have to see each other when they arrive in Coral Shore to prepare for my and @TheLRicci's wedding #CordukeReunion
@IrisLaArt
Cordelia is the maid of honor & Duke is the best man. She doesn't know it though. #CordukeReunion
@GKNYC
I don't know why she doesn't know; I swore I told her. #CordukeReunion @IrisLaArt
@JamesSheath
You never told her, none of us did, just like none of us told her about Duke' yearly Christmas visits. #CordukeReunion
@GKNYC
@IrisLaArt

Back on track now, when they're reunited for the first time, we expect tension, but we're also hoping to see if they still have the spark #CordukeReunion
@JamesSheath
They'll be engaged by the end of the weekend, guaranteed. #CordukeReunion
@IrisLaArt
I don't think so @JamesSheath, care to make a wager? #CordukeReunion
@JamesSheath
Sure, what are the terms? @IrisLaArt #CordukeReunion
@IrisLaArt
If they're engaged by this time next week, I will take you to dinner at that new place in SoHo you're dying to try. #CordukeReunion
@JamesSheath
And if they're not, I will take you to dinner at that place in Williamsburg that you love so much. #CordukeReunion

♥

Cordelia Watson knew she and her best friend Iris should've rented a car and just driven up, but Iris insisted this would be better. Maybe she didn't realize just how much stuff they would have to take up for the five or so days. So now Cordelia tried to make her way down the train car with her suitcase, garment bag, her purse and work bag.

Iris was already in their seats, her feet up as she ignored Cordelia's pleas for help. Iris packed lighter and planned to spend as much time in a bikini as possible; while Cordelia had to not only bake and decorate the wedding cake and bake a few other things her friends had grown to love. Plus being the Maid of Honor was no easy task.

7

The cake was why they were going up today anyway; Cordelia wanted to get it started tonight. She wanted to make sure it was done except for final touches before the Keller family chef took over the kitchen for the weekend. If things were going as planned Gage and Lauren wouldn't be at the house yet, it would just be Iris and Cordelia. It would give her time to focus on the cake without extra distractions.

"Iris, please will you hold this? It has all my cake supplies." Cordelia tried to hand her friend one of her bags while looking for a place to stow the others. Why had she agreed to the train ride? Why was it packed in the middle of the week?

Iris took the bag, focusing on her phone while she watched Cordelia start to fall backward and into someone's arms. She bit her lip to keep from smiling; she didn't have to ask who it was that caught her.

"Hey, do you need help?"

Cordelia froze when she heard his voice, her heart was about to leap out of her chest when she realized that his hands were on her again. This couldn't be, no way would he be on this train of all trains?

"I've got it, thank you." Her words were fast as she pulled away from him, afraid if she hadn't, she would've melted into him and made a huge fool of herself once again.

"Cordelia?" He looked around to see her face, a smile growing on his lips and in his peridot green eyes.

"Hi, Duke." She couldn't look at him, she wouldn't. Why had she not thought about this being possible, why hadn't Gage warned her?

Duke stood back and looked around to Cordelia to see that her companion was Iris. "Hi, Iris."

"Hey Duke, let me guess you're off to the big wedding this weekend huh?"

"Well, I am the best man." He wished Cordelia would look at him; he longed to see her barn wood brown eyes in person. "I guess I'll see you girls there, James and I are sitting back here."

Cordelia couldn't move until she was sure he was gone and not still right behind her, she could still feel the impression his fingers left on her skin. "Iris,"

"It's okay Cor, I mean of course he was going to be there this weekend, he's Gage's best friend." Iris looked at her phone for a moment, and then back up, "Wait, you did realize that Duke would be Gage's best man, didn't you?"

Cordelia shook her head, her shoulder length brown hair dancing on her shoulders, "I've been so busy helping Lauren, designing the cake, convincing Noah I didn't need a date for this, I didn't even think about who the best man was, or that Gage would ask Duke."

Iris looked at her friend, she knew it was going to be a long few days, "Listen, it's a big house, lots of stuff going on; I mean really how often are you going to have to see Duke? I mean you'll walk down the aisle with him after the ceremony, take a few pictures, maybe dance one dance, but that's nothing."

"You're right, it's a huge house. We've gotten lost in it. Remember that year we came up for the Fourth of July? We barely even saw each other." Cordelia thought back on that memory, James had been up with them. Somehow Cordelia barely saw either of them that weekend.

Iris leaned back, watching Cordelia, "What happened between you two anyway?"

Cordelia rubbed her left ring finger as she stared out the window, "Duke knows what he did Iris, Duke knows why I had to send him the promise ring back. It didn't feel right to keep it."

Still no answer, seriously what happened? "Just hide out in the kitchen making the most glorious wedding cake that Coral Shore are ever going to see, and when you're not there you'll be down at the beach with me. Maybe we'll meet a cute set of millionaires to whisk us off our feet."

Cordelia said nothing as she stared out the window, feeling a knot form in her stomach. It was only a matter of time before she had to see Duke, really face him, she wasn't sure she was ready for this.

"Iris, Cordelia, two of my favorite ladies, I have a favor to ask." James's voice was warm, but

Cordelia had a feeling she knew what he was about to ask. "A family of four wants to sit together, Duke and I were wondering we could sit with the two of you."

"Yeah, that's fine." Cordelia continued to look out the window, "Just James, you sit next to me, okay?"

"Whatever you say Butterscotch." He left to give Duke the okay.

"You going to be okay?" Iris tapped on her phone.

"I have to be." Cordelia could feel her stomach twisting into several knots.

♥

@IrisLaArt
#CordukeReunion has officially started, Cordelia literally fell into his arms on the train, I didn't even have to push her this time.

@IrisLaArt
She still says Duke knows why they broke up, he did something. #CordukeReunion

@GKNYC
Want to bet that their breakup was over some stupid misunderstanding, and Cordelia got insecure about something? #CordukeReunion @IrisLaArt

@IrisLaArt
It had to be something real @GKNYC, she wouldn't throw everything away over a misunderstanding. So yeah let's make a bet. #CordukeReunion

@GKNYC
If it's something real, I'll get your tickets to that musical you are dying to see. #CordukeReunion @IrisLaArt

@IrisLaArt
Oh, good one. Well if it's something ridiculous, I will give you that sculpture of mine you're always trying to buy from me. #CordukeReunion @GKNYC

@GKNYC
We've got a deal @IrisLaArt! #CordukeReunion
♥

James dragged Duke with him, forcing him to sit next to Iris, which gave him a chance to see Cordelia, watch as she stared out the window. James figured Cordelia hadn't thought about turning around and being able to see Duke. He didn't know what happened, he was positive that Duke didn't know either. He took his seat next to Cordelia, pulling out his phone, reading his twitter feed and realizing he'd missed a bet between Iris and Gage. He moved onto his emails.

"Hey Iris, I'm hearing the great buzz about your show next month." He tried to start a conversation, but sure he could handle the train ride and the strained silence that was vibrating from Cordelia.

"Really? I haven't finished, I have a piece I'm working on, but something is just not working. I'm hoping a few days away will help clear my head so when I get back, I can figure it out." Iris looked to Duke, "So, what are you up to these days?"

"I just got my Veterinarian License; I'm going to be starting a practice soon." He looked over to Cordelia, "What about you, what are you up to these days?"

"I run Beverly's, Mom got busy with the law firm; Dad is busy as Principle, so I took over." Her voice was flat as she continued to stare out the window, trying to remind herself to breathe.

Duke leaned back in his seat looking to Iris who just shrugged, followed by James doing the same thing, "We don't have to talk, silence is good, silence is nice."

"You would think that," Cordelia said softly, not realizing her words had been released to the world.

Iris and James didn't understand, but Duke knew that it was going to take a lot of work to get Cordelia to do anything more than play nice during their time together this week.

♥

@JamesSheath
Icy start to this #CordukeReunion, but I think things will melt quickly.
@IrisLaArt
I wouldn't be so sure of that, but I guess only time will tell @JamesSheath #CordukeReunion

♥

When the train arrived at their stop, Duke offered to help Cordelia with her bags, but she would only accept it from James. As he carried his own bags, he followed behind to stop Iris, "Why is she mad at me?"

"You broke her heart; you had to have done something Duke." Iris shook her head, "She says you know what you did."

"I didn't dump her, I didn't even suggest it, I was planning to propose to her over Christmas break." He confided in his old friend. "But she stopped talking to me, sent the promise ring back. She and I need to have a long talk, don't we?"

Iris looked up from her phone over towards James and Cordelia at the other end of the depot, "Yeah, you do, you two always need to talk."

Gage had left two cars at the station for them to use. The girls loaded into one, while the boys followed in the other.

As Cordelia drove the vocals of a country song filled the space and kept Iris from asking her the questions she didn't want to answer.

Iris turned the radio off as she looked at Cordelia in the driver's seat, "Who broke up with who?"

"Who are you talking about?" Cordelia flipped the radio back on.

Iris turned it off again, "Cordelia, you and Duke; who broke up with who?"

Cordelia held the steering wheel tightly, her knuckles turning white as she made her way down the road, "I broke up with him before he could break up with me. I was trying to protect myself."

"But why, you and Duke were crazy about each other." Iris left out the part about him planning to propose, but it was obvious that they each still carried a torch for the other.

"I had my reasons, okay. None of that matters, it was eight years ago. Why do you all keep asking about it? Duke knows what he did; Duke knows why we broke up." She took a deep breath, "This weekend is about Gage and Lauren, not me and Duke, okay?"

"Whatever you say." Iris turned the radio back on.

"Iris?" Cordelia started before glancing over at her friend, "Why do you think Duke and James were coming up today and not on Friday like everyone else?"

"No idea, you'll have to ask them. I'm sure they're wondering the same thing about us." Iris continued tapping on her phone.

♥

@IrisLaArt
Cordelia says she broke up w/ him so he wouldn't break up w/ her. Duke says he was going to pop the question that Christmas. #CordukeReunion
@GKNYC
He had a ring and everything, he even asked her Father for his blessing. @IrisLaArt #CordukeReunion

♥

"So, you and Cordelia, together, in the same place for the first time in how long?" James looked up from the tweet he'd been reading from Iris and Gage as Duke drove towards the Keller' house.

"Too long," he breathed, "She hates me, I still don't get it, James, what did I do?"

James slid his phone in his pocket, "Listen, as far as I know, she never told anyone why she stopped talking to you, why she sent the ring back, not me, not Iris, and not Gage."

"She really took over the bakery?" He realized she would be nearby, at least during the workday.

"Oh yeah, after college she went to culinary school to become a Pastry Chef."

"She did?" Duke kept his eyes on the car in front of him, following as it turned onto a long driveway, "Why didn't know any of this?"

"Because, it hurt too much to ask, I think." James pulled his phone back out when he felt it vibrate. "She's making the wedding cake, that's why she and Iris came up a few days early."

"Early, I thought you and Gage said everyone was arriving today?"

"Did we?" James wished the car was parked so he could jump out, "No, Gage wanted us to come up so the girls wouldn't be up here alone. You know how he worries."

"James, what are you and Gage up to?"

"Gage, Iris and I aren't up to anything." He realized his mistake as soon as her name passed over his lips.

Duke took a deep breath, "Iris is in on whatever scheme you've cooked up?"

"Duke, nothing is going on, we're not plotting anything."

He parked the car behind Cordelia, "She didn't know I was coming to the wedding, did she?"

"Nope, we all thought she would realize you would be here, that you would be the best man, but she didn't."

Duke watched Cordelia for a moment as she got out of the other car and started to unload her bags. Why did she have so many? "Cordelia, let me help you with those!" He called as he climbed out of the car.

"No, it's fine. I have this." She insisted as she almost fell over trying to balance everything.

"Cordelia, I can help you." He took her work bag and suitcase, following her into the house.

"Okay, Gage left a list of what rooms everyone is in." Iris announced as she looked at the piece of paper, "Well James, we're suitemates, you're in blue and I'm in red! Duke, you and Cordelia get the white and purple rooms."

"Wait, that can't be right Iris, let me see the paper." Cordelia reached for it, they'd spent enough time the last few summers in the house to know which rooms shared a bathroom and which didn't.

Iris handed her the paper, "It's true, it comes from his Mother; you know the one your Dad and Dennis call Monster."

Cordelia sighed, "Wonderful." This was going to be a very long week, she wasn't sure how she would get through it, and it was starting to feel like everyone was plotting against her now.

"James and I could trade, right? Mrs. Keller wouldn't be upset with that would she?" Duke suggests seeing how upset Cordelia was.

"Nope, she would, I'm sure she just wants the best man and maid of honor near each other for emergencies." James looked to Iris, "Let's go get settled, that great burger place isn't far from here, let's meet down here in say an hour and go to dinner, sound good?"

"Sounds great to me!" Iris grabbed James by the arm and the two disappeared before Cordelia or Duke could protest.

"They're setting us up," Duke told her.

"I was starting to think so." Cordelia grabbed her work bag and went towards the kitchen.

Duke followed, "Eventually we should talk, shouldn't we?"

"Why?"

"Because our best friend is getting married and we're important to him and his bride. Can we at least pretend to be the friends we once were, just until they cut the cake? After that you never have to talk to me again if you don't want to, how does that sound?"

Cordelia began unpacking her bag, "So basically a truce of sorts, let's give it a try. Just one rule, stay out of my way in the kitchen."

"As you wish, I'll go drop your bags off in your room, see you in a little bit." Duke smiled to her as he backed out of the large kitchen, how was he going to survive the next few days if she kept up this frosty behavior?

Cordelia was thankful to finally be alone as she unpacked her bag of baking and decorating tools, her hands shook. All she wanted to do was cry; release the flood of emotions building inside of her. She didn't have time, not now anyway. She could make it through dinner, and when they got back, she could take a hot show and then she could cry.

CHAPTER 2

Cordelia went upstairs to freshen up, she'd never stayed in the purple or white rooms before, in fact, she and Iris usually just shared one room. They'd only been in either once when Gage showed them around. That had been years ago before Jennifer Keller redecorated. She hadn't expected the plush purple room she entered. Duke had left her suitcase on the stand for her, hung her garment bag up on the door, and placed her purse on the chair.

Why did he have to be so well mannered? That made all this more difficult.

She took her makeup bag out from her suitcase opening the door to the bathroom; it fell from her hands as she saw Duke step out of the shower. "I am so sorry; I had no idea you were in here." She turned and ran out, shutting the door. Crap, they were sharing a bathroom.

"Cordelia, I'm done; you can do whatever you need in here," Duke called out from the other side of the door.

She opened the door peaking in, seeing him in the thick white towel around his waist, Holy God, he'd gotten even more muscular in the last eight years, hadn't he? "I forgot we were sharing a bathroom."

"It's okay Cordelia, I forgot about it as well. Let's just agree to lock the other door from now on so no one walks in on the other." He smiled, "Unless you want to walk in on me again."

"Duke Shaw get out now!" She threw a washcloth at him as he moved towards his door which she promptly locked behind him.

Her friends were scheming against her, probably for her, but right now it felt like they were ganging up on her. She thought for a moment and then realized that Iris and James would be sharing a bathroom as well, wondering how they were dealing with that.

She splashed cold water on her face, cleaning her makeup from earlier in the day off, scrubbing her face before she went for a simple coat of eyeliner, mascara and her favorite tinted lip-gloss. She brushed her shoulder length hair, missing her long locks for a moment.

"Cordelia, could I come in, I forgot something." Duke knocked against the door and she went to unlock it, letting him in.

"I'm done for now anyway." Cordelia tossed her things back in the makeup bag as she watched him move in his jeans and tight t-shirt. She couldn't help but wonder what it would be like to be crushed in his embrace against his chest.

"I like your hair." He called out.

Cordelia stopped in the doorway, turning to him, "Thanks, this is more practical these days for work."

"Well, it looks good that way." He wanted to run his fingers through her hair again, let him tease her as he massaged her neck, the way he would just before kissing her.

"I'll see you downstairs." Cordelia closed the door, leaning against it for a moment, trying to remove any and all thoughts of his body out of her mind.

She quickly changed into her favorite sundress, grabbing her cardigan for when they were out in the night air. As she pulled her hair back, she saw the chain she wore every day, it wasn't very long, most outfits it was hidden under, no one ever seemed to notice the small locket that lay next to her Greek letters. She pulled it up; Duke had given it to her for her sixteenth birthday, opening it for the first time in she didn't even know how long she saw younger versions of herself and Duke smiling, ready to take on the world, to live the happy lives together they expected.

It was only now that she wondered why she was still wearing it every day, why wasn't it in the box she kept under her bed of things that reminded her of him, things she couldn't part with. Why was she still wearing him close to her heart?

She didn't want to think about it as she let it slip back under the neckline of her shirt and she grabbed her purse. ♥

Iris and James were both staring at their phones as they sat at the bottom of the steps waiting for her with Duke.

"Sorry to make everyone wait," She stopped, "Iris, James are we going to have to invoke the phone rule?"

They sighed and handed their phones to Cordelia who slipped them in her purse.

"Duke, your phone please." She held her hand out to him.

"Are you serious?" He took his phone from his back pocket.

"Very much so, in case you didn't notice these two barely look up from their phones, so in it goes." She could feel the warmth of his hand when he placed the phone in hers. Quickly she pulled her hand away, dropping his phone in her bag.

"Well then, let's go. This is going to be so much fun." James sighed.

"Oh please, it's not the worst thing to happen to you today."

James looked to her, "Iris . . ."

"What, they share a bathroom as well, so what I accidentally walked in on you. It's not like you have something I haven't seen before." She batted knowing eyes at him.

"Iris!" James snapped his eyes drilling into her.

"Sorry." She brushed it off as she looked towards Cordelia and Duke, "You know James, I have a feeling dinner is going to be very interesting."

"Oh no, when you say that nothing good happens." He told her as she leaned in close to him.

"Listen, you distract them, I'll get our phones and then we'll ditch them, so they have to walk home." She told him her plan, "And as they walk, they talk, maybe if we're lucky they clear the air tonight rather than us having to scheme a million other ways to get them to talk."

"You sure about this?" He opened the car door for her.

"Positive, it has to work."

♥

@GKNYC
Waiting to hear how the room assignments went, but I'm betting Cordelia took everyone's phone so @IrisLaArt & @JamesSheath looked up from their screens. #CordukeReunion

♥

The weeknight crowd was more locals than tourists, which meant things, were a bit calmer and allowed the group to talk without shouting over each other.

"So, I'm at this performance art show, and this woman takes a bottle of chocolate sauce and starts screaming 'BOSCO, BOSCO!' like she was George Castanza or something," James explained the most recent piece he'd reviewed for the site NYCBuzz.com an entertainment and life site.

"Do you go to a lot of those?" Duke was curious, he knew what James's job had been for the last few years after an ankle injury forced him to give up dancing.

"Yeah, I'm probably out at shows, gosh, Iris how many did we see last week?"

"Five, we went to five." She took a sip of her margarita and looked around.

"And you have a gallery show coming up right? Gage was telling me about it."

"Yeah, I have everything, but one piece figured out. But I still have time, so I'm not too stressed yet, and if I do get stressed, I always know I can get one of Cordelia's fresh baked batches of cookies if I need them." She tried to lead things back to Cordelia who sat silently, already caught up on most of this stuff with her friends.

Duke turned to her, flashing his smile that always made her toes curl, even now it did, "So Cordelia, how is the bakery business?"

"It's wonderful, there's this group of high schoolers, they come in every morning, even now that it's summer. They can just sit and talk for hours . . ." Suddenly she realized who they reminded her of. "My mornings won't be as bright when they all go off to college in the fall."

"That's a shame."

"So, what have you been doing in Texas, I'm sure it wasn't all school." She could feel her fingers trembling as she kept her hands on the table so no one would notice.

"Mostly it was school, in college it was classes and the Zeta's, and occasionally I would Rodeo, I'm still the Master of Tombstone."

"That's something to be very proud of." She rubbed her left ring finger focusing on that rather than looking up at Duke, knowing those green eyes of his would cause her to get lost.

James began an animated story about a graffiti artist he'd met recently, distracting Cordelia and Duke long enough for Iris to get the phones and slip them into her bag along with the car keys.

"I'll be right back." Iris excused herself, hoping that James would realize it was time a moment later to excuse himself as well. She paid the bill, keeping an eye on him. She took her phone out, snapping a picture of Cordelia and Duke together, she was trying not to look at him, while all he could do was look towards her, they slowly finished their drinks.

"Think it will work?" James asked when he found himself next to her.

"It better." Iris took his hand, fingers interlacing. "Let's go, besides if they have to walk home that gives us time alone."

"Oh, was there something you wanted to do, alone with me."

"Maybe, or maybe not." Iris began tapping away at her phone as they went out to the parking lot.

♥

@IrisLaArt
This is getting painful to witness. Just talk already, hash it out, have hate sex, do something! #CordukeReunion

@GKNYC
That does look painful, but I don't think either of them are hate sex people. @IrisLaArt

@IrisLaArt
Okay @GKNYC, they're probably cheesy love song, candles and roses people. Happy now? #CordukeReunion

@GKNYC
Let me know if I win the bet @IrisLaArt ;) #CordukeReunion

@JamesSheath
They're probably walking back from dinner right now, fingers crossed they finally talk. #CordukeReunion

@GKNYC
Why are they walking home from dinner? What did you 2 do? @IrisLaArt @JamesSheath #CordukeReunion

@IrisLaArt
Took the phones, car, paid, and left them no choice but a moonlit walk on the beach. @GKNYC #CordukeReunion

♥

"Iris should be back by now." Cordelia reached into her purse for a pack of gum when she noticed that the four very important devices were missing. She bit the inside of her cheek to keep from cursing.

"Where did James go?" He asked, wondering why she looked angry this time.

"Home, they took the phones and the keys and went home." Cordelia shook her head before picking up her wine glass and taking a large sip.

26

Duke watched her, "I mean we can get a cab, right?"

"That'll cost too much." She felt around again, "She took my wallet."

"I have cash." He reached for his and pulled out the worn piece of brown leather.

"Really Duke how cliché." Cordelia rolled her eyes as she looked away from him.

"What?" Looked down to see what she was upset about, the only thing possible could be the circle worn in the leather, "It's not what you think Cordelia."

"Let's just walk home, it'll be faster anyway." She picked up her sweater, throwing it over her shoulders as they went to pay, finding the bill already taken care of. Thank God for small favors Cordelia thought.

Duke followed behind her; he couldn't help but think she was adorable when she was mad, at least not at him. Of course, he also loved that she saw the worn circle on his wallet and thought it was a condom. It was too small, even if he carried one around with him. Yes, he had a stash, he was pretty sure they weren't expired, but he couldn't tell anyone the last time he looked. He hadn't needed once since the last time he was with Cordelia.

"I should've known Iris and James were up to something." Cordelia finally spits out as they stepped onto the beach.

"Why is that?" Duke caught up with her quickly, fascinated by the way the moonlight reflected on her hair.

"They gave up the phones with very little fight; they always fight me on it." She trekked along quickly.

"Cordelia." Duke stopped walking and waited for her to turn around.

"What?"

"Slow down; enjoy the beach, the sound of the waves." He walked towards her, "Yell at me, tell me off, tell me what I did so wrong eight years ago. Tell me why you sent the promise ring back." He hadn't meant to go straight for it, but they might as well hash it out now.

"We were freshmen in college Duke, you were making new friends; I was making new friends, we were at different schools. We were with different people and we were changing, people change people."

"The secret of life," He finished, "Cordelia was there someone else?"

"Not for me, but I know Duke, I know about her."

He stepped towards her, what in the world was she talking about? "Who?"

"Your Texas girlfriend, the one you obviously found the first week of school."

"There was no Texas girlfriend, you were my girlfriend. The only girlfriend, I gave you a promise ring, and I meant my promise. You just stopped talking to me, you stopped answering my calls, emails, texts, video chats, and then one day I checked my mailbox and there it was, the ring."

She could feel the years of pent up anger, frustration and curiosity starting to bubble through her, "Who was Wanda?" Crossing her arms over her chest she looked up into his eyes, thankful it was dark enough out right now she could keep herself from melting from that peridot gaze.

"Wanda?" Duke had to think for a moment, "That goat?"

"Goat?"

"I was pledging my fraternity, and they had a pet goat, Wanda. I had to take care of her."

Cordelia sank down into the sand, "A goat, I thought a goat was a girl you were cheating on me with. Wow, I am a moron."

Duke sat next to her, she wouldn't look at him, and finally, he spoke: "I'm still confused about how you got this idea in your head."

"The last video chat," She breathed as she looked towards the water, she couldn't fathom looking at him right now, "You didn't hang up, you were in a rush or something. I don't know, and just as I was hanging up, I heard your roommate say something about you having a hot date with Wanda."

Duke didn't know if he should yell, or cry, or laugh, "Why didn't you confront me? Why just stop talking and send the ring back to me?"

Cordelia buried her feet in the sand, wishing she could bury her head right now, "I was devastated, I was taking a few days to calm down, and then I saw pictures of you with a girl on Facebook, and thinking back their might have been a goat in the pictures."

"Wanda the goat," Duke leaned back in the sand, clapping his hands, "I lost the love of my life because of a goat."

"What did you say?" Cordelia felt her heartbeat quicken; no, he didn't do that. We are not going there.

Duke sat up, taking her hand in his, "That I lost the love of my life because of a goat."

Cordelia didn't know what to say, she felt ridiculous, a goat, Wanda had been a goat. She slipped her hand from his and rose, "We should keep walking; the house is still a bit away."

Duke sighed as he stood, walking the few steps behind her for a few minutes before allowing himself to catch up with her, "So, baking, how did you discover a talent for that? Did you work at the bakery over the summers?"

"No, actually it was when I was living in my sorority house." She smiled at the memory, "We would have little bake-offs that the guys from the ZGN house would vote on. I had a winning streak for a while until they forced me to retire. It took me a while I guess, but I finally found my thing. Funny how it was so close to me and I never suspected."

"I'm really happy for you Cordelia, I knew you would." He couldn't help but wonder if she dated any of the fraternity brothers, "Wait, Zeta Gamma Nu guys?"

"Yeah, anyways when I graduated with my business degree, I knew that wasn't really what I wanted. So, I came back to New York, went to culinary school to become a pastry chef. When I graduated, I started taking over the bakery, slowly at first and then before I knew it, it was mine." She pulled her sweater tightly around her shoulders as the cool breeze came off the ocean.

Duke stepped towards her, wrapping his arms around her, "You always get cold out; it's seventy-five degrees and you're shivering."

Cordelia wanted to object to the feel of his arms around her, while they were the arms she remembered, the ones that haunted her dreams during her early morning sleep, they were different. They were thicker, more defined with his muscles; he either finally started working on his strength or he spent a lot of time on the ranch still.

"So, are you going to start a practice in Austin?" She pulled away from him she knew the house wasn't much further.

"Actually; no not in Austin." He stopped himself from telling her he was going to be opening a practice in New York. He followed her, she didn't want him to break through to her, it should be easy now that he knew why she ended thing, but it wasn't.

"You'll do fine wherever you end up." Cordelia turned to him and immediately she realized it was a mistake. Seeing him now in the moonlight, this was worse than the first time she saw him on the subway. Time was good to him, oh so very good. "What about your girlfriend, I'm sure she has something to say about where you end up."

"Don't have one; I've been single for a very long time." He threw his hands up, why wasn't she getting this? "What about your boyfriend, I'm sure he misses you. Will he be at the wedding?"

Cordelia was caught off guard, why did he care if she had a boyfriend? "Oh um, I don't exactly have a boyfriend. Occasionally I do go out to dinner with Noah."

"Noah Wilson?" Duke felt the jealousy boil through his body.

Cordelia smiled, she knew that would get him, and it made her happier than she realized to find that out. "Yeah, he's making a boatload of money on Wall Street these days, always trying to woo me. I feel bad every now and then, so I let him take me to dinner or a show."

"Of all the men in New York, you're dating Noah Wilson?" Duke wanted to hit something, throw something, but even more than that he wanted to kiss Cordelia, erase any memory of Noah from her, reboot all her memories of them, together.

"Oh look, we're back." She tried to change the subject as they approached the private beach.

"We're not done talking Cordelia." Duke moved quickly to catch up with her on the steps of the deck, his hands landing on her shoulders as she spun to look at him, "Why Noah?"

She focused on his eyebrows so she wouldn't get lost in his eyes, "Duke, you are making this a much bigger deal then it is, besides what was I supposed to do, just wait around hoping that a Rodeo Star from Texas was going to show up and sweep his Princess off her feet again? Isn't it time to let go of silly dreams? Besides I thought you cheated on me."

Duke didn't know what to say to her, he just let himself get lost in the dark brown eyes; she was scared, he just wasn't sure of what yet. He was going to find out though.

"We should really get in the house, no telling how many rooms Iris and James are bold enough to have sex in if we're not home."

Duke dropped his hands from her as he stared at her, "What?"

"They're hooking up, have been for years. Its top secret, they haven't told anyone."

"Ha-ha, funny, Iris tells you everything." Duke followed her up the ocean spray worn steps.

"Not everything," Cordelia thought of that first summer when she'd returned home from school. They were so different, they had changed so much, "We kind of grew apart in college if we didn't come up here every summer with Gage, I don't know if we'd still be friends."

"What happened between you girls?"

"Nothing happened, we just started making new friends and well you know the secret of life."

Cordelia shrugged, "Iris was in the art crowd, galleries and older men, parties till dawn. I was a sorority girl; I was President of my chapter senior year."

"Gamma Gamma Nu President huh?"

"How did you know?"

"You mentioned ZGN brothers, Zeta Gamma Nu, chapter President senior year." He smiled.

"So, you dated Gamma Gamma girls huh?"

"When I dated," He confessed, but really, he had only dated when he needed a date to the formals or other events. None of it had been serious, and after college, he focused on graduate school, working the ranch for his Grandfather. No girl had ever gotten to him the way Cordelia had.

"So, you're totally like my brother then." Cordelia teased, seeing him flare just as he had moments ago when she brought up Noah.

"Don't start with the bullshit Cordelia."

She had never heard him curse before, "Well, goodnight Duke, I'm going to give Iris a piece of my mind if she's not doing whatever with James."

"Are you sure they're hooking up?"

Cordelia looked out to the other side of the beach, "Watch them, you'll see. I don't know when it started, but the last few months, it's been pretty consistent."

"I guess I've missed a lot."

"Yeah well, I'm sure you'll miss even more when you go back to Texas." Cordelia started to race up the steps, she was done talking to him right now. She had to go; she couldn't let herself get lost in him before she knew the truth. She just hoped the picture that had caused her to send the ring back was still on Facebook. She had to know if she made the biggest mistake of her life—over a goat.

Duke watched as she raced up the steps, Texas . . . she thought he was going back to Texas to start his practice. That explained some of this; he would wait to tell her; he would see if he could get through to her first.

"Why is Cordelia saying, 'a damn goat' over and over to herself?" Iris had come from the house looking for Duke, finding him sitting on the steps staring out into the dark ocean.

"What do you know about why Cordelia and I broke up?" He looked up at his old friend.

Iris thought for a moment, "She never told us, all she has ever said is Duke knows what he did. But we always got the impression you have no idea. I do remember her saying you have a new girlfriend, but when I saw you at Christmas, I knew that couldn't be true, you were all about Cordelia."

"Did she ever mention the name of that girlfriend she thought I had?"

"Wanda, I remember thinking it's a cool name, but lousy on you for moving on, but that was again before I actually saw you."

Duke rested his head in his hands, "Wanda was a goat I had to take care of as part of my

Fraternity pledge. I lost Cordelia over a goat. I didn't even know she thought I had another girlfriend until twenty minutes ago."

"So, you really never knew why you broke up."

"Nope." Duke rubbed his face, "She just stopped contact, I knew she was mad about something. I was getting ready to drive up to Colorado when the ring arrived."

"That damn promise ring." Iris sighed, "So wait, somehow Cordelia got it in her head you were dating a girl named Wanda, but it was really a goat you were taking care of, how?"

"I don't even know, she said something about Facebook."

Iris slapped him on the shoulder, "Well Duke, go look at your Facebook pictures from back then you got tagged in. It's probably still up, right?"

"Maybe, I have no idea." Duke looked up at the house; he could see the light on in Cordelia's room. "How serious are things with her and Noah?"

It took Iris a moment to realize what he was asking, "Wait did she tell you that she and Noah are dating?"

"Yeah, all the men in New York and she dates Noah Wilson." He tried not to say anything else.

"Hold it, Duke, they're not dating." Iris could see the jealous fire burning in his eyes, how had she missed that in middle school? "This just getter and better, James and I should make popcorn for this."

"What do you mean they're not dating?"

"Okay, so here's the thing. Cordelia hasn't dated anyone since she moved back to New York, she barely has time. She keeps the most ridiculous hours at the bakery. I bet if you go down to the kitchen at say one, you'll find her just starting to bake the cakes. She'll sleep from like nine in the morning until three in the afternoon. She does her errands or whatever, and then goes to the bakery for the night shift, works all through the night."

"Why would she tell me she's dating Noah if she's not?"

"Well Duke, every so often Cordelia realizes she hasn't gone out beside me dragging her out to an art show, or James to one of the wacky plays he has to review, or maybe Gage drags her to a seminar. So, Noah comes into the bakery every night when he gets off work and asks her out. So maybe once a month she says yes, if that. It's nothing serious; I don't think they've kissed."

"What about in college, didn't she date guys in the Frat?"

Iris shrugged, "I mean I think only when she had stuff, she needed a date to. I don't know how any of that works; Cordelia was born to be a sorority girl, me, not so much."

"Do you think I have a chance with her still?"

Iris looked down at her hands, twisting the friendship ring Cordelia had given her in middle school, "If you're serious about her, yes, I think you do, I think the world could use a Corduke Reunion."

"I'm serious Iris."

"What about Texas, don't you live there?" She asked wondering what he would say.

Duke rose, looking out towards the water, "I need a drink."

Iris watched him walk away; it was going to be a long week. She just hoped that they could get as much of the anger and tension done before Gage and Lauren arrived.

♥

"Cordelia?" James called out as he followed her up the stairs; he was always surprised how steady she was on her feet these days, "Butterscotch!"

Cordelia stopped in front of her room. "What?"

"What's going on? Did you and Duke clear the air?"

"Almost, I have to check something." Cordelia paused before opening the door, "James, did Duke ever tell you about Wanda?"

James tried to remember, "Wasn't that the name of his Frat's goat, he had to cart it around and call it his girlfriend during pledge or something?"

Cordelia bit down on her lip, "Let's find out."

"Wait, why?" James followed her into the room, watching as she pulled her laptop out of her bag, her foot tapping nervously as she waited for it to wake up and connect to the Wi-Fi.

"Because, if Wanda is really a goat; then I made a huge mistake." She placed the laptop on the dresser, typing Duke' name into the search, scanning the page for his photos before she started a journey back eight years. One thing she noticed was the lack of females in his photos in the last few years.

James watched her, "Cordelia, why does it matter now?"

"Because James, I need to know if I messed everything up over a goat, a Taylor Swift belting goat." She ran her fingers through her hair, dropping them as she saw the picture, "This is it."

James moved close and watched it enlarge on the screen. It was a picture of Duke, a goat, and a blond girl. Shit, no wonder Cordelia freaked seeing this; he wouldn't assume it meant the goat.

Duke Shaw with his girlfriend Wanda.

Cordelia hoovered the mouse over the girl in the picture, she was tagged, Claudia Adams. Why hadn't she done that eight years ago? She hovered the mouse over the goat, Wanda. She closed the laptop and looked at James, "I dumped him over a goat."

James pulled her into a hug, feeling her tears dampen the shoulder of his t-shirt, "It's okay, mistakes happen, goats happen. You know the truth now; you'll figure out how to accept it and move on."

"I told him I'm dating Noah," Cordelia confessed as she enjoyed the embrace of one of her friends.

James started to laugh, "Cordelia that is going to drive him crazy."

"I know, I think if he could've kicked a sandcastle down, he would've." Cordelia wiped her tears with the ball of her hand as a sensation of calm came over her, "Do you think, well, you know, it's possible?"

"You two getting back together?" James looked at her, how had Duke not fought for this girl?

"I mean I know he lives in Texas, and I don't think I could let the bakery go, but do you think he even maybe wants that?"

"I'm going to be honest with you Cordelia; I've kept this from you for years." James took a deep breath, "It killed him when you sent that ring back and wouldn't talk to him. He survived, he threw himself into school and the Frat, just as you did with the Sorority. He survived losing you, but a future; I think a reunion between you two depends on if you guys can even talk. Do I think that spark is still there? Sure, I do. But you have to be open to it."

"Thanks, James." Cordelia sat down on her bed, "Oh one more thing."

"What?"

"You and Iris, what's going on between you two?"

James's eyes were wide, "Nothing, we're just friends."

"James, I see the way you look at her, I see the way the two of you touch each other when you think no one will notice."

"Iris and I are great friends, Butterscotch; I'm going to let you figure this stuff out. Just don't beat yourself up too much over this goat thing."

"Easier said than done, and you should figure out your stuff with Iris."

"We're just friend," he reminded her as he backed out of the way, "Cordelia, follow your heart. When you don't, that's when you get into trouble."

♥

@IrisLaArt
Okay @GKNYC you can pick the sculpture up when you get back from your honeymoon. #CordukeReunion

@GKNYC
Wait you found out why they broke up! Details woman! Don't Belgium 1831 me! @IrisLaArt #CordukeReunion

@IrisLaArt
It's so stupid, but Cordelia dumped Duke because she thought he got a new GF @ School named Wanda. @GKNYC @JamesSheath #CordukeReunion

@JamesSheath
Why the hell would she think that? @IrisLaArt @GKNYC #CordukeReunion

@IrisLaArt
It gets better...Wanda was a goat Duke had to take care of for Frat Pledge. #CordukeReunion @GKNYC @JamesSheath

@GKNYC
A Goat... a goat... a goat? #CordukeReunion @IrisLaArt @JamesSheath
@JamesSheath
A GOAT?! #CordukeReunion @IrisLaArt @GKNYC
@IrisLaArt
Found the picture; kind of don't blame her, would you think someone meant the goat! @GKNYC @JamesSheath

♥

"Cordelia thinks something is going on between us." James put his kindle down on the nightstand as he watched Iris come out of the bathroom in her nightshirt. "She told me to figure out what this was."

Iris snorted, "Yeah, cause she's one to talk."

"A goat, she thought some stupid goat was Duke girlfriend at school."

"I know, how ridiculous. I mean I saw the picture, I found it after I talked to Duke, I get it, but still, she just stopped talking to him, sent the ring back." Iris lay next to James on the bed, "He was going to go see her when it showed up."

"Do you think they'll get back together; do you think they should?"

"No idea, he did get awfully upset about her saying she's dating Noah." Iris snuggled closer to James as he put his arm around her.

"She did that for the reaction."

She raised her eyebrow as she looked to him, "Did she get the reaction she wanted?"

"I think so." James pulled her in closer to him, "I think we can safely believe that they're going to get back together, I have no idea if it'll work. Then again, he will be living right next door to her."

"She's going to freak when she finds out." Iris smiled, "You don't think they'll actually like look up our tweets from this week, do you?"

"Cordelia sticks to Instagram and when was the last time, she didn't post a cake? Duke is a Facebook guy; I don't think either of them has tweeted since college."

James watched as Iris pulled up her twitter feed on her phone.

@IrisLaArt
Can't wait to hear from Cordelia all about the goat, wait does this mean I lost the bet @GKNYC? #CordukeReunion

"If they find out about these tweets, they might kill us."

"So, it's for fun, for us, and really at the end of the day who is even going to know it's them?" Iris put her phone down before lying back next to James, hers fingers lightly dancing on his chest.

James's fingers played with her hair before he kissed her, every single time they kissed he was surprised by the jolt of energy he felt. If anyone had ever predicted that this would happen between him and Iris, he would tell them they were crazy.

CHAPTER 3

Cordelia took a shower, making sure the door to Duke's room was locked tight. She didn't know if he'd gone back to it or not, and right now she didn't care. She couldn't deal with him walking in on her. She just wanted to wash the day away, pull her hair back and spend the late hours of the evening baking.

She needed to bake, she needed to create a delicious sweet batter, she needed to work. She needed to get out of her head, and into her meditative state, she didn't want to think about Duke anymore tonight, she didn't want to think about how Wanda had been a goat he was taking care of, an honest to God tin can eating goat. Did goats really eat tin cans? Cordelia picked up her phone to google it but felt silly. The answer was on the other side of the door, she could knock, but then she realized how late it was. He was probably asleep right now, like every other normal person on the planet.

She made sure the bathroom door was unlocked for him before she pulled her hair up into a bun and left for the kitchen.

She flipped the lights on and started to gather her ingredients, preheat the oven and get set up. She was thankful that the house was so large she wouldn't wake anyone up with the noise of the mixer.

When she set the oven, she glanced at the time, it was half past midnight. She would have this place all to herself. She enjoyed late night baking; that was part of why she worked the hours she did, why she stayed up all night. It gave her a sense of calm, something that for a while had been missing in her life.

♥

Duke watched from the deck as Cordelia moved around the kitchen, she knew this one well and he wasn't surprised. They all spent time in the summers here. Obviously, she had done her late-night baking here before. He kicked himself for not fighting for her then; he wanted to give her space. Why had he been so stupid?

He took a sip of his beer, watching as she put the cake pans in the oven, and then started to clean up her first project. She had flour on her face and in her hair, she looked more beautiful then he'd ever seen her look before.

He realized the bottle was empty, so he just sat watching her chop strawberries and then some nuts, he couldn't tell what they were from where he was sitting. He saw her stop, roll her eyes as she picked up her phone.

He couldn't just sit around any longer, he rose knowing he could use the time difference as an excuse for being up, but she might not believe it. But he could tell by the way her eyes crinkled she wasn't enjoying her late-night phone call.

"Noah, I told you I really don't need a date for Gage's wedding. I'm very busy helping Lauren get ready for her big day." She had her back to Duke not knowing he was there, "You want to know why I don't need you to be my date Noah; because Duke Shaw is my date."

He smiled, he couldn't help it, and he knew that would drive Noah probably just as mad as it would've Duke in the reverse situation.

"Noah, I'm sorry, Duke is my date for the wedding . . . You don't believe me?"

Duke grabbed her phone from her, "Noah Wilson, it's really late don't you think?"

Cordelia couldn't help but be thankful that Duke had taken the phone from her, but what was he doing here in the kitchen this late at night?

"Listen, Cordelia and I will be attending Gage's wedding together, as a couple. No, I did hear that you occasionally go out to dinner, but Noah, New York is full of women looking for your special brand of romance." Duke rolled his eyes, "Cordelia and I are back together, we had a very long talk on the beach tonight. When I looked in her barn wood brown eyes, I knew I couldn't live the rest of my life without her. I'm sorry buddy, but you know I'm sure you'll find someone else, night."

"Thank you." Cordelia accepted the phone and slipped it into her pocket, "You didn't have to do that, but it gives me a few days without him."

He pushed some hair from her eyes, "No problem, I never liked that guy."

"I know," She flashed on a memory of his jealousy when they were younger, "It's going to be really awkward when he finds out you and I aren't back together, he'll show up at my apartment with flowers, tell me that he would never break my heart and run off to Texas."

Duke frowned, "Actually, I think we've established I didn't break your heart."

"I should apologize." She gave him a smile before clearing her throat before she started to sing, "I'm sorry for treating you so bad."

"Adorable," He smiled, "I would love for us to talk about this, but I get that you're busy right now. I was just enjoying the summer night air; I saw you looked upset on the phone. I wanted to make sure you were okay."

"Just Noah, being, Noah, at the very least I have about a week or two free of him."

"If you don't like him, why go out with him?"

Cordelia looked away, afraid to get lost in his green eyes, "Same reason I did in middle school."

"Well just one thing," He watched as she started chopping nuts again. "Don't make a liar out of me, be my date for the wedding."

"Duke, we don't need dates. We're in the wedding party." She could feel the nervous energy he'd always created bubbling inside of her again.

"Just think about it." He didn't want to leave her; he wanted to spend as much time with her as he could, even if he was a distraction. "What are you making?"

"These are for some muffins for the morning; fresh muffins are a tradition here." She looked up long enough for her eyes to lock with his.

"So that's what I've been missing out on by coming up the two weeks after you." Duke refused to break her gaze, "Yes, I've still been coming here every summer. I came the other two weeks so I wouldn't crowd you, plus I didn't want to see you with any of your boyfriends."

"I've never brought a boyfriend up here Duke," She looked back down at the nuts as she continued to chop them.

Duke watched as she moved towards the pantry, and God help him he followed, "Not even Noah?"

"No, not even Noah; part of why he called at almost two in the morning trying to be my date." She could feel her hands shaking when she realized how close he was, he smelled amazing, but she couldn't place the scent, it was like fresh ocean air, a good microbrew, and something else, probably just his pure scent.

"I almost feel bad for him, almost." He smirked.

"Why do you care?" She looked up at him, knowing she could get lost in his green eyes for the rest of her life, she'd always known that but now she knew it, she understood the kind of pain it could bring her when she didn't have them to be lost in.

Duke continued to lean against the doorway, taking the large canister of flour from her, "Because you deserve way better than Noah. Does he still just pop up out of nowhere, that was always creepy."

"I'm not actually dating Noah." She confessed as she moved past him with some ingredients.

He smiled, "Good."

"I found the picture." She told him taking the canister from him with ease before she began measuring her ingredients into a large bowl.

"Oh, you did huh?" He pulled himself up to sit on the counter, watching her.

She nodded as she continued to work, "Yeah, I'm sorry I let some ridiculous misunderstanding come between us. I'm sorry I stopped talking to you, I'm sorry that I let that end us."

"Apology accepted" Yes, Duke was making progress, "I'm sorry too, I'm sorry I didn't fight for us the way I should have. I'm sorry I didn't get in my truck and drive up to see you like I planned to do. I'm sorry that we never spoke, I'm sorry that I haven't seen you in far too long."

Cordelia looked up at him, "You were going to come to see me?"

Duke nodded, "Yeah, I was packing my bag, I couldn't take that you weren't talking to me, ignoring my calls and emails. So, I was all set to drive up to Colorado. Find you at the dorms and find out what was going on."

"And then you got the ring."

"And then I got the ring."

"I'm sorry I sent it back, it was a beautiful ring." She smiled as she thought of the silver band with stars on it, sometimes if she let herself, she could still feel it on her finger, "Whatever happened to it? You pawn it in a fit of anger, or no it's sitting in the back of a drawer somewhere, or you don't even know. It's probably in a box you haven't opened in ages."

"It's somewhere safe, I promise."

Cordelia rolled her eyes, "What are you doing up this late?"

"It's an hour earlier for me; you know I'm from Texas after all." He watched her smile fade, "Besides, I could ask you the same thing. Why are you baking this late?"

"This is what I do." She held her hands up as she looked around the kitchen, "If I were in New York right now, I would be in my kitchen at the bakery, I would have all kinds of stuff going, getting ready for the morning, getting ready for the day. I sleep in the mornings, my manager comes in around eight, and then I leave."

"Do you still live with your parents?" He already knew the answer.

"No, but my apartment is in the building. Mom bought it a few years ago, she rented out the other retail space a few months ago, but whoever got it has been doing some major construction. Apparently, they'll be in the apartment next time mine." She glanced at the timer on the oven, "I like being close to the bakery, and this really great one bedroom opened up, so I took it. It doesn't have a bay window though, but that's okay."

"Where do you and Iris talk then?"

"Usually her loft, actually she doesn't come by very much. I usually go to her." Cordelia had never realized that before, when had that started?

"So how are your parents?" Again, he knew the answer; he'd seen them just that morning. He'd had a nice chat with Mr. Watson when he picked up his keys and gotten the building's security code.

"Good, Dad's still teaching, and he's the Principal now. Mom's the senior partner at the law firm, Steve is off in college broke up with Gabi much to my mom's relief."

"I'm sorry to hear that." Duke watched her, "Are you making what I think you're making?"

"What do you think I'm making?" She studied him, watching as he jumped from his position on the counter and started to take over her ingredients, "Excuse me, Shaw, what are you doing?"

"I worked at the bakery; I know what I'm doing."

"Duke, helping my mom out behind the counter once in a while isn't working at the bakery."

"I know, but that first summer after college I came back to New York, I worked at the bakery every day I could. I kept hoping you would come home, that your internship would end early and I would see you."

Cordelia watched as he added the ingredients perfectly, "I never knew, no one told me."

"Well, now you know." He started to knead the dough as he watched her, she was impressed.

Don't get distracted by his muscles. Don't get distracted by those green eyes. Don't get distracted by him. He'll go back to Texas on Monday. You've cleared the air; just don't fall for him again. Don't open yourself up for the heartbreak that is bound to come from Duke Shaw.

The timer went off and she took the cakes out of the oven, set them aside before putting the muffins in, she turned the radio on, hoping it would break the silence that it would distract her from Duke who didn't appear to be heading to bed anytime soon.

"So, do you know where you'll set up your practice?" She started to wipe down some counters, she needed to be busy. Usually this time of night she was, but this was simple and the added energy she felt having him so close wasn't helping her right now.

"Yeah, I got the space a few months ago from an old family friend. It's great; I'll have the clinic and my apartment in the same spot." He finished kneading the dough, setting it aside to rise. "If I'm lucky, I might even have room for a bunny farm."

"Shut up, do you know how much trouble I got in when my Dad found all those bunnies in my room?" She shook her head, wondering what she'd been thinking at the time. She hadn't realized just what would happen when she had so many bunnies together, she jumped in and gotten over her head.

"I thought it was adorable." He soaped his hands up at the sink washing them.

Cordelia was trying to find something to say, and then she heard it. That song, of all songs in the entire world, this one was playing at two am.

"Cor, come on, we have to." He reached out for her hand.

"We shouldn't Duke."

"Come on, it's playing for a reason." He felt her fingers in the palm of his hand, pulling her body towards him. God, it felt good to be this close to her after all these years.

Cordelia let herself melt into him, close her eyes and pretend that the last eight years of nothing between them never happened.

"How did this ever become our song?" She was afraid to look up, positive he held her tighter.

"I think you found it on one of your mom's CDs."

Cordelia let herself give into the sensation, the complete calmness that was enveloped around her as they slow danced in the kitchen. No one would ever believe this.

Duke couldn't remember the last time he'd heard this song. It had been old when they picked it as theirs. Once they had, it was on every playlist they ever made each other.

Cordelia realized she was in trouble when the song ended. Knowing now that he hadn't cheated on her in college; that Wanda had been a goat let her unlock the padlock she'd had on her heart, and the moment she did Duke was right back there.

The oven timer went off and she took the muffins out, placing them to cool and turning the oven off. Suddenly the kitchen was far too hot for her, she needed air.

She said nothing and walked out towards the beach.

Duke followed, grabbing the battery-operated lantern that sat by the door. "Cordelia where are you going?"

"I just need air, Duke." She could feel her heart pounding in her chest. God why couldn't he leave her alone, why did he have to be so damn close?

"What are you afraid of Cordelia?" He was behind her; she could see the light from the lantern washing over them.

"After this weekend, you go back to your life and I return to mine. We live in very different worlds, Duke. I lost you eight years ago because I was beyond stupid, but I was also scared. We weren't together, video chats, texts, those aren't the same." She turned to him, "Everything inside of me is yelling for me to kiss you. But my brain knows that once we step foot on that train Monday afternoon, it's done."

Duke understood what she was afraid of now. He got it. He understood. "Give me this week."

"What?"

He planted the lantern in the sand and walked towards her, his hand slid up to cup her face, "You and me this week. If you want to kiss me, kiss me. If I want to kiss you, I kiss you. If you want more from me, you get more. If you want me to wrap my arms around you and fall asleep with you in them, well damn it Cordelia that is exactly what you are going to get. If you want to slow dance in the kitchen in the middle of the night while we wait for something in the oven, I will dance with you. You just want to sit on the sand and listen to the waves crashing then we'll do that.

"This weekend, here in Coral Shore, Cordelia and Duke reunited. We don't have to tell anyone; it can be a secret. We can be friendly in front of everyone, and alone . . ." His hand slides down her throat, towards her neckline, he could feel her heartbeat.

"If I said I wanted you to make love to me tonight, while the bread is rising, while the cakes and muffins are cooling in the kitchen, you would make love to me?"

"Your wish is my command." His voice contained a growl, he wasn't sure how much longer he could be this close to her and not kiss her.

"Kiss me." She breathed, afraid he wouldn't, afraid she was about to wake up from the daydream.

Duke' lips crashed down on hers with a hunger she remembered and hadn't felt in far too long. His hands moved over her body as she stretched her long frame to fit with his.

He dreamed of kissing her again, he remembered kissing her, but this was different, years of loss due to a misunderstanding drove him with need.

Cordelia pulled away first, afraid if she didn't, she would never stop kissing him. "No one can know. This is our secret." Her fingers interlaced with his.

"Our secret, Cordelia and Duke one last Coral Shore week together." He tried to catch his breath as he looked at her, this week, he could do that, he would do whatever he could to make her happy this week. Whatever happened after Monday afternoon would be a different story altogether. He would worry about that later.

Cordelia's free hand began to play with the chain of her locket, she wanted to say something to him, but the words that were about to come out were ones she didn't dare say out loud to him. "Come to bed with me."

"Are you sure?" He asked as she started to lead him up the deck steps, grabbing the lantern.

"If we have this time together here, then I want everything I can get from you." They stopped on the stairs.

Duke kissed her, "As you wish my Princess."

♥

They turned the lights and radio off in the kitchen, Cordelia led him up the stairs to her room. She was nervous, she hadn't been with anyone, well since the last time she was with him. She'd gotten close a few times in college, but it never felt right.

Duke felt right.

Duke never thought he'd have another night with Cordelia, they hadn't had very many, to begin with, but those nights had been special. Cordelia was the only woman he'd ever been with, no one else could compare to her. If she just wanted this time in Coral Shore, she would get it, and he would do everything he could to show her how good they were together.

Cordelia turned the bedside light on, slipping out of her shoes. She watched as Duke removed his t-shirt with one hand that magical way that men do. She reached out touching his chest, dear God it was everything she remembered and everything she'd dreamed of.

Duke felt her touch as red hot and it drove him wild, he reached to her, removing her shirt, finding her with a sports bra on underneath. He pulled that off as well, there they were both shirtless. She was just as perky and curvy as he remembered.

They kissed again, neither knowing if Cordelia jumped and wrapped her legs around him or if he pulled her up. He moved them towards the bed, he wanted to go slow, explore everything, but another part of him wasn't sure he could.

He moved to taste her neck; she arched her body towards him. He laid her back on the bed, kissing her, kneading her breasts, his thumbs teasing her nipples to hard nubs before he suckled them. God, he'd missed this, her, everything. A few days in Coral Shore wouldn't be enough; it could never be enough for him, but it was a start.

Cordelia was pretty sure she was going to orgasm already, and he'd barely started to touch her. How did he have this effect on her? She reached down, unbuttoning his jeans, pulling the zipper down, and just wanting to touch him, finding the silky, hard, erection waiting for her.

"Cordelia," He gasped when he felt her touch, and then pulled away long enough to remove his jeans and boxer briefs. Before he returned to her, he pulled her pants away, leaving her in just her panties for a moment, his fingers traced the area around her cotton briefs. She would never believe how sexy she looked right now if he told her.

She gasped when she felt his fingers inside of her; it had been too long, far too long since he'd touched her. God, she was addicted to it already, how was she going to survive without this? Get as much of him as she could this week, that's how.

He watched her body move with his touch, the way her eyes fluttered; her fingers gripped the sheets, the way her muscles twisted in response to his touch.

Fuck she was sexy.

He kissed her knees, her thighs before he buried his face in the hot, wet, desire he created in her. He could feel her legs tighten around his head as he licked her up with all the hunger, he'd had for the last few years. When she came, it just encouraged him to continue.

"Duke . . . Oh God . . . what are you . . . oh, that . . . Duke . . . fu . . ." Her words became the sounds of pure passion released and a moment afterward she felt Duke pull away.

"Do you have a condom?" He asked, trying to remember if he thought to pack any.

"No, don't you?"

"Maybe, I don't know." He rushed into the bathroom, going through his things, hoping to find one, but he never carried them, he never needed them. He pulled through a few drawers and found one, "Got it." He called out before he returned to the bedroom, watching her try to sit up dizzy with pleasure.

Cordelia watched as he ripped the package open, slipping it on his long shaft. It wasn't until right now she realized how much she needed him, needed his touch, needed to feel his breath on her all this time.

Duke sat on the bed next to her, kissing her, feeling her move on top his lap, feeling himself enter her. This was it, this was heaven, they moved together, their bodies connected, and he didn't want it to end, "You feel so good Cordelia."

She held him tight, sensing it would be soon, memories of the handful of times they'd been together soaring through her, never had it been this good.

"Oh Cordelia," He moaned as he picked up the pace, feeling her body shudder with her own climax at the same time.

Their bodies coated in sweat, the heat of their long-held back desire, the summer morning, they glistened in the rosy light.

Cordelia didn't move, too afraid it would be over; just the most erotic daydream if she did.

"We should shower." Duke kissed her neck.

"Good idea." She didn't move, and before she knew it, he was holding her tight as he stood up, carrying her into the bathroom, "Duke, what are you doing?"

"We're going to shower, why do it alone when we can do it together?" He asked setting her on her feet in the walk-in shower before turning on the water spray.

♥

It was four in the morning; Cordelia knew by the light outside coming in the bathroom window as Duke made love to her in the shower. They'd never done that before, but it was amazing. She wanted all her showers to be like this from now on, if only.

Afterward, she towel-dried her hair, putting it in a braid before getting dressed again. Duke changed into a pair of gray sweats and a blue t-shirt. Every chance he got he touched her, kissed her, if she wasn't insisting on going back down to the kitchen right now, he would make love to her again.

So, he followed her down, not wanting to lose any time with her. He kneaded the bread dough while she removed the cakes from their pans, setting them up to go in the walk-in freezer. He set the dough aside to rise again and put the radio on. Hoping another slow song would fill the room and he could dance with her.

When Cordelia returned from the freezer Duke took her hand as a new song started.

Duke held her close as they danced again; he could smell the fresh scent of her shampoo in her still damp hair, his fingers slipped under her shirt, trying to memorize the feel of her skin against his fingers.

Another slow song came on and Duke held her close, he wouldn't stop dancing with her until he had to.

Cordelia let herself enjoy the feel of Duke against her, holding her, dancing with her. She wished this could last forever, and every time she did, she remembered that it would have to end eventually, but that was still so many days away.

"So, tell me what your daily routine is like." She pulled away when a DJ came on to deliver the headlines and weather.

He couldn't keep his eyes off her, "Well, it had been getting up at 5:30, usually helping out at the ranch before I had to go to the clinic where I've been working for a few hours, and then studying."

"I heard you stayed on Tombstone a full five seconds." She went to the Keurig and popped in a pod for coffee, pulled out a mug from the cabinet.

"You did keep tabs on me, didn't you?"

She looked away, "James told me all about it. Might have been one of those times they were trying to find out what happened between us. See how I would react to hearing about you."

"Well, it wasn't the same without you there to cheer me on." He watched her, trying to figure out what she was thinking.

She pushed the brew button and turned to him, "Are you going to continue to Rodeo?"

"No, it was fun, especially when I got to impress this gorgeous brunette from the big apple, but I don't have that drive or stupidity to keep doing it."

Cordelia blushed as she pulled another mug down and grabbed another coffee pod, "Still drink it black?"

"Yeah, I do; thanks." He took the full mug from her, he could get far too used to this, but then again it wouldn't be like this would it? No, she would be in the bakery, working, they wouldn't have lazy mornings together.

He watched as Cordelia doctored her coffee with some flavored creamer and a bit of sugar. Somethings never changed.

"Are you excited to start your own practice? I know I was excited, nervous, terrified when I took over the bakery."

"I am, but I think the location I got is going to be perfect."

"Well, they'll be lucky to have you, Dr. Shaw."

"Wow."

"What?"

"No one's called me that before, it's kind of weird." He set the mug down on the counter, "You want to go watch the tide as the sunrises? Iris and James will probably still be asleep for a while."

"That sounds perfect."

♥

Iris shook James awake, "What's wrong?"

"Cordelia didn't come to vent about Duke, I'm worried." Iris crawled into the bed lying next to him; they'd agreed to sleep in separate beds so she could be available to talk if Cordelia needed her.

"That's good, though right?"

"What if she's in her room crying because, I don't know, he said something stupid."

James took her hand, pulling her closer to him. "Iris, she was probably baking or staring out at the ocean. Duke wouldn't even know where to find her; he doesn't know her wacky schedule."

"I told him she bakes late at night." She looked down.

"Oh, well maybe they talked, maybe they're okay."

"What if this Corduke Reunion thing is a total bust?" She relaxed when she felt his arms wrap around her.

"Then we'll have really ridiculous tweets for the three of us to laugh at."

"You sure they don't tweet?"

"Yes, when's the last time a tweet came from Cordelia's account that wasn't an Instagram post? I think the last time Duke tweeted was something about his frat back in college." He kissed her temple, "Get some sleep, it's still early. The sun isn't even up yet."

Iris closed her eyes, relaxing as she felt James planting soft kissing along her hairline.

♥

Duke had grabbed a blanket from the house before they'd gone out, he wrapped it around them as they sat in the sand, watching as the tide pulled out and the sun crept over the far-off horizon of the ocean. When he looked down at her, he got lost in how magical she appeared in the early morning sun, he kissed her.

Cordelia sighed into the kiss; this was everything she'd missed, everything she needed in life. How could she give this up now? Because he would be gone before she knew it.

Duke pulled her onto his lap, kissing her neck, "Cordelia . . . you're the only woman—."

"Shh, Duke don't talk." Cordelia pressed her finger to his lips, "Just do, just kiss me, touch me, make love to me right now."

"I don't have a condom." He got lost in her eyes, now a golden brown with the rising sunlight.

Cordelia reached into her jacket pocket and pulled one out, "I came prepared, it was the last one in the box though."

Duke took it from her fingers; "I'll get more later today." he kissed her before breaking away, the condom wrapper between his teeth as he took the blanket and laid it on the sand before laying Cordelia down beneath him.

They kissed, slowly, pulling away from their clothes that blocked their access to each other before he slipped the condom on and made love to her as the water hit the sand, the sun rose to greet the day. Moments like this, with Cordelia, would always be memorable. The way her fingers dug into hard muscles, the way she reacted to his touches, the sounds she made begging for more.

Cordelia held onto this moment, she needed it to last forever. Making love with Duke on the beach during sunrise, how as any of this possible? Less than twenty-four hours ago she didn't even think it was possible to be in the same room with him, let alone feel his touch again.

She moaned his name into his ear as she climaxed, biting down on his shoulder to keep from saying anything else she knew was trying to burst out.

Duke lost himself when he heard her breath his name. He didn't even notice her biting into him.

It wasn't until they were putting their clothes back on that Cordelia noticed.

"Oh no, I think I did that." She studied the mark she'd let, "Teeth marks, crap."

"I'll put a band-aid over it, no one will notice really." Duke wasn't sure a band-aid on his shoulder would go unnoticed, but he figured something out if it didn't work.

Cordelia lifted the blanket, shaking the sand from it, "I should probably get that bread in the oven, Iris and James will probably be up soon."

"If they're not distracted by their own romp," Duke joked, "Why do you think they're denying it?"

Cordelia shrugged as she folded the blanket and Duke collected their shoes, shaking the sand from them. "Iris got really hurt in the past, so has James. I don't even know when they started this, it could be something new and they're not ready, or it could be something they've been doing for years and are afraid of admitting."

"Years, you really think so?" Duke followed her, taking the blanket when he caught up.

Cordelia turned looking out at the ocean, a smile on her lips, "I mean think about it. For four years when we were all in college, it was just the two of them in New York. Gage was in Cambridge at MIT, you were in Texas, I was in Colorado. Sure, we all came home but, they bonded. I mean they've dated other people over the years, but honestly, it always seemed like Iris was trying to distract herself from someone, I used to think it was Blake, but the pasts few weeks I've been thinking it was James."

"Always the romantic, huh?"

"I guess some things never change."

Duke took her chin in his fingers, "Don't let that go Cordelia."

"Duke the bread." She smiled before bounding up the deck steps.

He stayed on the steps for a moment watching her drop the shoes by the door, spraying her feet with the outdoor shower, and then draping the blanket over the side of the deck.

♥

@JamesSheath
Time to find out if #CordukeReunion will happen or not, fingers crossed they've calmed down about #TheGoat

♥

James put his phone down as he looked at Iris asleep next to him, "Hey, I think I smell fresh bread, you know what that means."

"Breakfast! Cordelia baked us goodies." She snuggled close to him, breathing in that scent of his, a mix of his cologne and body wash, it was unmistakably him. No other man could combine those two products and smell this good.

"We should go downstairs; we might have to keep them in separate corners," James warned her.

"They're exhausting, can't we return them?" Iris whined, not wanting to get up.

James laughed, "Nope, we're stuck with them for life, just one more day of doing this just us, besides once everyone else arrives, they'll be distracted; Maid of Honor, Best Man kind of stuff."

"Good point." Iris sat up, knowing she had to get up, "Besides, today Cordelia promised to lay in the sand with me."

"Now that's a plan I can get into."

"You would think that." Iris went to the door, "I'll see you in a few minutes."

♥

"Cordelia, come one," Duke told her as the song came on the radio; she was setting the table while he'd been making a fruit salad.

She took his hand, and he twirled her around the kitchen. The song was old, but Cordelia had always felt a special connection to it, and it seemed Duke had as well.

"You remember how much I love this song huh?" She felt her body cash against his, and it took everything for her to not kiss him.

Duke smiled as he looked into her brown eyes, "I remember a lot of things Cor."

Iris and James stood back; they could hear the song, but they couldn't believe their eyes. Iris aimed her phone towards them, taking a quick snapshot and then a quick video of the two of them dancing.

"Think they talked?" James couldn't believe his eyes.

"If not, this song is pure magic, look at them. When's the last time you saw a smile like that on either of them?"

"Way too long." He looked at her, "Update time?"

"Already on it."

♥

@IrisLaArt

#CordukeReunion update, look who we found dancing in the kitchen together. Shh, they don't know, we know.

♥

Iris's phone rang with a vibration in her hand shortly after the tweet was sent. She saw Gage's

69

face on the caller ID and grabbed James, pulling him into the Library before answering it, "Hey, what's up?"

"They're dancing together, and someone explains the goat thing." He asked in the hyper way that only he could pull off.

Iris closed the door and put him on speaker phone, "Okay, so here's the deal. Apparently, our darling Cordelia got upset over a picture one of the Frat guys posted of Duke, and the caption said, "Duke Shaw and his girlfriend Wanda.""

"Ouch."

"It was a goat-man; Wanda was a goat." James couldn't help but laugh when he said it, "The goat has a Facebook page, but there was a girl in the picture, she was tagged, but Cordelia overreacted."

"This is why she sent him the promise ring back, over a goat; oh, my sweet, silly Cordelia." They could hear the amusement in his voice, "Now one, this means I win the bet and two, how did they end up dancing in the kitchen, was it just because it was that song?"

"Maybe, we don't know. We were about to go into the kitchen when a curious pal called." Iris rolled her eyes.

"Okay, okay, find out. Keep me updated. By the way, have you guys been checking your mentions? People are kind of into this."

"Really, who besides us would be interested?"

"No idea, just be careful." Gage sighed, "I gotta go; Lauren and I will be there tomorrow with my parents, Cordelia's and yours Iris."

"Great, we'll see you then." Iris hung up, "Okay, let's find out what we can."

Cordelia heard the door of the library open, she looked up pulling away from Duke when she saw Iris and James come out, "Morning you two, what-cha doing?"

"Just answering a phone call, Gage wanted to check in. They'll be here tomorrow with our families." Iris slipped her phone in her pocket, "You two, what's going on here?"

"Nothing at all Iris; just making breakfast." Cordelia pushed her friend towards the Keurig, "Have a cup, we've got the strawberry walnut muffins you guys love so much, some fresh bread, and Duke made a fruit salad."

"You let him in here while you were baking?" James followed Iris, something was up, but he wasn't sure what.

"I mean the bread was in the oven, everything else was done. He wasn't in the way." Cordelia could feel her hands shaking as she went to the table. "I had the kitchen all to myself all night, it was a perfect evening."

"So, did you two, talk?" Iris dug through the collection of coffee pods looking for her preferred brand.

"We agreed to let the past be the past, right Cor? We're here for Gage and Lauren, we can be civil, we're adults." Duke brought a bowl of fruit salad and a pitcher of orange juice to the table.

Cordelia sat in her favorite seat, picking up a muffin, watching everyone gather, "So, how did you sleep Iris, James?"

Iris found herself choking on her juice, "I'm sorry, what?"

"How did you sleep; I know sometimes you have trouble when we leave the city."

"Oh, um, I slept fine. I woke up worried that you hadn't come to vent, but I see you didn't need to."

"I'm sure you did." Cordelia split her muffin with her fingers, she was now convinced that Iris spent at least part of the night in bed with James.

"What about you Duke, how did you sleep?" Iris wanted the attention off her.

"I couldn't sleep, I tossed and turned in the bed a bit, took a walk on the beach, watched the sunrise." He bit into his muffin hoping that Iris left this alone.

"James, want to check out some galleries with me in town this morning. I know Cordelia will go to bed soon and sounds like Duke needs to try and sleep as well."

"What about spending the day lying in the sand?"

"We can do that this afternoon, after Cordelia gets some rest. You know her wacky sleep schedule, which really Cinnamon you've got to do something about."

"I'm only going to sleep a little while this morning, I promise. I want to get sort of normal before the wedding." Cordelia took her plate to the sink, "In fact, I think I'm going to go get some sleep right now. I'll see you in a few hours."

It took every ounce of strength that Duke had not to go after her, not follow right behind her on those stairs and crawl into bed with her, to just hold her as she fell asleep.

"Why does she keep such odd hours?" He looked at his friends.

"No idea, Beverly and my Mother said she didn't have to get the baking done like that. But I guess it just works for her. Good thing she lives in that apartment a few floors above the bakery."

"Not far from her parents either."

"They'll always be close; Steve even works for her part-time, helping when he can. He's probably driving the manager crazy right about now." James watched his friend, "So you two didn't talk or anything?"

"Just enough to agree to try and get along and for me to tell Noah to back off."

"Wait for what?"

"Okay, so I came in at two, and he had called her and was I guess begging to be her date for the wedding, she told him I was her date, she didn't know I was behind her," Duke smiled, "So I took the phone and told him to find another girl."

"Okay, you just won some major points, Duke. Hopefully, that guy finally gives up." Iris took a sip of her coffee. "You know I could've sworn I heard Daydream Believer when we were coming down the stairs, was I wrong?"

Duke sighed, "No, it came on the radio. Listen, I'm going to try and sleep. You guys have fun at the galleries, okay?"

"Yeah, good luck." Iris called out, watching him leave, "James, they lied to us. Something is going on."

"Or maybe he couldn't sleep, and she baked all night. Maybe we want to believe something is happening, maybe the dance was just a moment between ex-lovers. Maybe they don't want us getting our hopes up, or theirs."

"Maybe," Iris picked at the muffin, "I'll drop it, for now, you really are going to the galleries with me."

"I'm fine with that."

♥

Cordelia changed into her pajama shorts and a tank top. She removed her braids and brushed her hair out; she brushed her teeth and with each little thing she grew anxious. What if he didn't come to her room, what if he didn't come to bed?

"Hi." He poked his head in from the bathroom.

"Hi."

"Hey." God, he felt like a middle schooler again, okay maybe not really but a part of him did. "I didn't know if you wanted me to follow, but I also didn't want to jump right after you."

"I'm glad you followed." Cordelia sat on the bed, the sheets a mess from their earlier time together, "Join me."

Duke played with the ends of her hair when he sat down next to her, "I really do like your hair."

"I like the way you touch my hair." She covered his hand with hers, "But I really do need to sleep, and so do you."

"I just want to hold you."

"Then hold me." Cordelia scooted across the bed to the other side, making room for him next to her.

Duke wrapped his arms around her, pulling her close to him, she smelled like fresh bread and the ocean. Her body close to his like this was heaven on earth as far as he was concerned.

Cordelia felt her body relax against him, falling asleep easily.

CHAPTER 4

Iris and James returned earlier than they expected from the galleries, curious about what the plan for the afternoon was.

James knocked on Duke's door when he got back, but when his friend didn't answer he let himself in. Duke's bed was empty and still made up perfectly, looking like no one had slept in it, no one had tried to sleep in it.

He went to find Iris in her room having changed into her bikini, "So, either Duke is an expert bed maker, or he didn't sleep in his bed at all."

"That's weird." Iris was pulling her hair up into a bun after having changed into her swimsuit.

"Yeah, maybe he couldn't sleep still." James pondered as he looked out the window. "Oh, he and Cordelia are down on the beach."

"She's up already?" Iris was shocked as she joined him at the window, seeing her best friend walking in the sand picking up seashells with Duke.

"This is weird right; they're collecting shells together now?"

"It's Cordelia and Duke, is it really that weird?"

"True." Iris sat on the bed, "What if we're wrong, what if they don't get back together. I mean she doesn't know that he's going to live next door to her, run his clinic out of the same building. Are you sure we shouldn't tell her?"

"They'll figure this out. They're grownups now, not scared college kids." James tried to rationalize everything, "Listen, Cordelia and Duke have never made this easy, they always want to play by their own rules. Whatever they may be, so if Duke needs for her to not know that he's moving back to New York, then so be it."

♥

"You know they're back." Cordelia sat on the sand, looking out into the ocean.

"Yeah, they're watching us. I just saw them from the window." He sighed as he sat next to her, "I'm sad our alone time is ending."

"We've had hours and hours of alone time, and we'll have more tonight. You can sit with me while I made flowers out of modeling chocolate if you want."

"That sounds perfect." He confessed; it really did. He would stay up all night; every night with her if that was the only way he got to spend time with her.

Cordelia rose from the sand, stretching, "I'm going to get something to drink, want anything?"

"I'll come with you. I want to check what we have, James and I were thinking of grilling tonight, and I promised Gage I would make him some Texas Style Barbeque tomorrow."

"Oh, now that will be a treat." She grabbed her bucket of shells and they started up the deck stairs.

Iris and James were sitting on the kitchen island waiting for them, "So collect some nice shells?"

"We're at the beach, what do you expect us to do? Not enjoy it?" Duke asked as he opened the fridge taking out a pitcher of lemonade for Cordelia and taking a quick inventory of what they had, which wasn't much, and he hadn't expected it to be stocked much with all the food that would be catered this weekend.

"Oh no," Cordelia was panicked as she dug through her workbag, "Damn it, I forgot it. How did I forget that stuff?"

"Cinnamon, what's wrong?"

Cordelia ran her hands through her hair, "The modeling chocolate, my airbrush supplies, I left them in my office."

"Call Beverly up and have her bring them tomorrow."

"I need to do the modeling chocolate tonight." She started pacing waving her hands in front of her face.

"Cordelia, calm down," Duke grabbed her by the shoulders and forced her to look at him. "We can make the modeling chocolate okay. Just tell me what you need; I'll get it for you. You can airbrush them tomorrow, right?"

"Yeah, I was going to anyways." She wanted to hug him, but she knew she couldn't with James and Iris in the room. "Thank you."

"As you wish," Duke pulled away from her, "You need the melts and corn syrup, right?"

"Yes, the white ones."

Duke pulled his phone out and typed it into a list. "James, come with me. We're going to grill tonight and gotta prep for the Barbeque for Gage."

"Sure, girls we'll see you later."

Iris waited until the guys were out the front door before looking to Cordelia, "He's still in love with you."

"He lives in Texas Iris; it would never work."

"Interesting."

"What is?" Cordelia looked up from her phone as she finished texting her mother.

"You didn't deny he's in love with you."

"Because I don't have to deny it, he's not in love with me, how could Duke Shaw ever love me after I dumped him for thinking he was cheating on me with a goat."

"Because he never stopped loving you, and you never stopped loving him, and you thought the goat was a girl." Iris took Cordelia's phone, "Look at me Cor, don't close yourself off from him."

"I'm not; we're trying to be friends again. That's all we can be, after this weekend I may never see Duke Shaw again."

"And that's the last thing you want in this world, isn't it?"

"It's how it is Iris, could I have my phone back? I really need those supplies."

Iris slapped it into Cordelia's hands, why was her friend being so difficult? Sure, Duke might technically still live in Texas, but he was moving back, coming home. "Figure out how to make it real then Cor, I know you never stopped loving him. I know you hoped every New Year's Eve he would show up on your roof."

"He was always gone by then." She realized sadly.

"Maybe you should've checked your fire escape on Christmas Eve." Iris let slip.

Cordelia placed her phone on the counter, "What does that mean?"

"Ask Duke, I'm sure he can explain it far better than I ever could. I only heard about it second hand anyway, maybe I'm wrong."

"Let's go lay out in the sun, how does that sound?"

"It sounds perfect." Iris followed her friend to the deck, collecting some blankets to bring down to the sand.

♥

Duke pushed the cart through the supermarket as James barely looked up from his phone, "What's so interesting that you've got your face practically glued to that thing?"

"Nothing that would interest you, I promise."

"Dirty texts from Iris?"

"No, Iris would never send me stuff like that." James grew hot with embarrassment.

"Yeah, sure she wouldn't." Duke grabbed some ribs and chicken from the butcher department, "Seriously James, are you guys hooking up, or something else?"

James looked up from his phone, "Iris and I are friends, we have a bond that the rest of you can't understand since you were all gone. We've seen wild nights, crazy art, stuff like that. We just have a slightly different look at the world."

"How long James?"

"How long what Duke?"

"James?"

He rolled his eyes as he followed Duke down the aisles, "It was this one time in freshmen year of college. It was Valentine's Day and she saw Blake with this girl, she was upset and I told her that Blake was an idiot if he couldn't see how beautiful she is, we kissed and next thing you know James has lost his V-Card and we never talked about it."

"Was that the only time?" Duke had a feeling there was more to the story.

James tossed a few items into the cart, "Sophomore year when I was upset about a girl, I had been dating it happened again. And we didn't talk for a few months. Then we ran into each other one night at a party and for the next few months whenever we saw each other, you know."

"I get the picture." Duke stopped the cart, "If you love her, tell her. Figure out what's going on between the two of you."

"Look who's talking, how many years did you climb up Cordelia's fire escape Duke?"

"Damn it, Gage, what else did he tell you?"

James slipped his phone in his back pocket, "Well, I heard you rented a nice little apartment in Greenwich Village, right by some great retail space, and near an adorable bakery."

"I didn't know she ran the bakery."

"Or lived in the building."

Duke sighed as he started to gather the stuff Cordelia needed.

"You really think she needs that much?"

"I don't know, but I don't want her freaking out at midnight because she doesn't have enough stuff." Duke couldn't help but smile though, figuring she might be kind of cute as she panicked.

"Duke, man, you are one of my best friends, you are my best friend, but so is Cordelia. I'm glad you two cleared the air and all, but dude she thinks you're going back to Texas. Tell her the truth, she's fragile, maybe you two can figure out a way to be together."

"I thought about telling her, it's crossed my mind a million times already in less than twenty-four hours. I need Cordelia to be willing to open up to me again, to give me a small chance, Monday she thinks I go back to Texas, and technically I do, to get my stuff."

"So, you're going to let her think you're leaving for forever, and then what you pop up as her new next-door neighbor a few days later?"

"Something like that." Duke shrugged as he turned down the pharmacy aisle.

"You're playing with fire, man."

"Yeah, I know. Cordelia is like a fire during a summer rain." He grabbed a box of condoms when James wasn't looking, and a moment later that James grabbed one as well. "You and Iris should have a talk."

"I don't know why we would, that was a long time ago." James was already back to looking at his phone.

"Whatever you say," Duke pushed the cart towards the next aisle, wondering why things were so complicated for all of them.

♥

@JamesSheath
"Cordelia is like a fire during a summer rain." Yeah, this fool isn't head over heels for her or anything. #CordukeReunion
@GKNYC

Interesting way for him to see her, I kind of get it though.
#CordukeReunion @JamesSheath
@JamesSheath
He's got it bad for her, even after all these years. He even
told Cheese Soufflé that they were back together. @GKNYC
#CordukeReunion
@GKNYC
Wait, how did that happen? Did he call her again asking to
come as her date? #CordukeReunion @JamesSheath
@JamesSheath
Yeah, late at night, she was telling him Duke was her date,
he overheard, took the phone told him they were back
together. @GKNYC #CordukeReunion
@GKNYC
You know he never liked Cheese Soufflé, so that was
probably a bit of fun. @JamesSheath #CordukeReunion
@GKNYC
Where the heck is @IrisLaArt w/ a #CordukeReunion update,
I was sure she would be on top of this.
@IrisLaArt
Currently enjoying bestie time on the beach, check out the
view. No #CordukeReunion news to report on this end. Sorry
boys. xoxoxo

♥

"Cordelia, did you and Duke ever sleep together?"
Iris asked as they lay on the blankets in the sand,
the afternoon sun beating down on their sun
screened bodies.

"Yeah, prom night and a handful of other
times." Cordelia thought of this morning in bed,
the shower, not far from here on the sand, "Why?"

"I just realized that I didn't know if you
ever did, I know you never have with Noah, and
the guys you dated in college were never very
serious."

"I'm not a virgin Iris, as cliché as prom night was, it was still amazing." She smiled at the memory, "He got us a small room at the hotel, he'd checked in earlier in the day and he put rose petals all over the bed, set up flameless candles, he had sparkling cider waiting on ice. We went slow, exploring each other's bodies for the first time. I don't know why I never told you that."

"Probably out of fear your father would hear and kill Duke." Iris sat up to take a drink of water.

"What about you, who did you lose yours too?"

Iris froze, she could remember that Valentine's Day night well. "This guy I was seeing in college," her mind flashed with memories of kissing James that night, of needing more then she'd had. "We had a little thing, but it ended not long after."

Cordelia had a feeling her friend wasn't telling her everything, "Iris, I know we're not as close as we once were. I don't know if it's that we grew up and changed a bit, or we just grew apart, but you can tell me anything."

"I know, and the same goes for you."

Cordelia lay back down in the sand, "Do you remember that movie, where the couple was married to different people, but for like this one weekend a year they would meet up and it was just them, together, falling deeper in love, living for that short time together?"

Iris looked to her best friend, her sunglasses pushed back in her hair, "Cordelia that is ridiculous, those people were having an affair. You can't live your whole life on the hope of a single weekend a year."

"I know that I just wanted to know if you remembered that movie."

"Cordelia, I remember, and I don't think it ended well. I think someone got hurt."

"But Iris, what if, you know what never mind. It would never happen, he's not going to keep coming up here each year, and really how many more summers will we make it up here ourselves?"

"As many as the Keller family will allow." Iris watched her best friend, wondering if having Duke around had just thrown her into a tailspin. "Gage is always going to let us come up here, so will his parents. We've been coming up here every summer since we were fifteen when they bought the place. Sure, we only make it up for a week or two now, and the occasional weekends, but we're building our careers, and someday we'll be able to come up more."

"You're right, it's our own lives keeping us from spending every day of the summer here, it would be nice if we could, maybe if we ever win the lottery." Cordelia looked out to the water, "I'm not going out to dinner with Noah anymore."

"For real, you're going to let the Cheese Soufflé deflate?"

"He called last night, late, but he knew I would be up. He wanted to come up and be my date for the wedding, I um, I told him that Duke was my date." Cordelia confessed she could see the smile creeping over her best friend's face. "And then, Duke took my phone from me."

"He did what?" Iris already knew, but she couldn't let Cordelia know that.

"Yeah, I guess he overheard what was going on and that Noah didn't believe me, so he told Noah we were back together, we'd cleared the air and Cordelia and Duke were a couple again and would be attending the wedding as such." Cordelia's cheeks were red as she spoke of the memory.

"Did you like that idea, being back together with Duke?"

"Loved it," Cordelia thought of how amazing it had felt when they kissed and then later when they'd made love. "But he'll be gone soon. So, I'm just going to enjoy getting to know him again. I mean it's been eight years, I'm sure he doesn't have the exact same dreams and goals he had then. I know I don't. Maybe, I need these next few days to become friends with Duke again, so that I can move on, to someone new."

Iris knew her friend was lying, she could never move on from Duke, if she had been able to none of this would be an issue right now. "Except for that one week a year where you plan to meet up with him and have a torrid love affair."

Something on Cordelia's face gave away that she was really considering that idea, "Yeah except for that Iris."

"Hey ladies, we've got lunch!" James called from the top of the deck stairs.

Cordelia got up, gathering her stuff. "Iris, you coming or not?"

"In a minute" She waited until Cordelia was gone before she gathered her things.

James was waiting for her at the top of the stairs, "Hey, you okay?"

"Yeah, maybe too much sun, not enough water." Iris was haunted by what Cordelia had just said.

"I found something out."

"What could you have possibly found out?"

"He doesn't want to tell her he's moving back to the city."

"Why that's so stupid, I swear I'm going to have to beat down Duke."

James grabbed her waist, "Wait, he has a reason and I think it makes sense. He wants Cordelia to open up to him again, not pressure her, right?"

"I guess." Iris felt her heartbeat race as his fingers danced on her skin, "What else?"

"Condoms."

"Great, we needed some, so?"

"I'm not the only one that grabbed a box."

Iris's mouth hung open, "Wait so he knows you bought a box, great they already think we're sleeping together."

"Iris, it means Duke bought a box as well. I don't know if he's just trying to be prepared or what."

"Does Duke really think he can seduce Cordelia this weekend, and then break her heart? Is that his plan?"

James held Iris tightly, "Trust me Sugar; he has no intention of hurting her. As I said, he could just be hopeful and cautious."

"Maybe," Iris couldn't get her conversation with Cordelia out of her mind, "I think Cordelia is going to propose something really stupid to him."

"Like what?"

"She randomly brought up this movie we saw years ago, about this couple that has an affair by meeting up once a year. I think she might suggest something like that to him. Like they pick a place and time to meet up, and no matter who they're with or what they're doing they spend that week or whatever together."

"Iris, she can suggest it, Duke can agree to it, but you and I both know he's coming back to New York. Besides, do you really think Cordelia would really suggest that; our Cordelia?"

"I didn't think she would break up with Duke over a goat, but she did."

"No one ever thinks a goat will come between a couple. We should get inside, they're suspicious enough don't you think?"

"James." Iris stopped him, "We're doing the right things, right?"

"We're doing what we do. Why?"

"Just nervous about them."

"Don't worry about it Sugar." He kissed her forehead with a quick peck before leading her towards the kitchen.

♥

"I didn't know how much you needed, so I bought everything I could," Duke told her as he handed Cordelia the takeout box.

"Did you get that item we discussed?" She looked around to see James and Iris have what appeared to be an intense conversation on the deck.

"Yes, and I noticed that someone else picked up the same item."

Cordelia's eyes shot wide open, "I knew it, did you ask him about it?"

"I'll tell you later." He nodded towards the door which slides open with Iris and James entering.

Over lunch they laughed about old times, talking about some of the things they had going on that the others might not be aware of.

"Iris has her first big art show coming up, don't you Iris?"

"I do, thanks for the reminder I've been trying not to think about it. I still have a piece to complete." Iris glanced over to James.

"You will, you always figure it out." James didn't think as he reached for her hand, taking it in his, his thumb rubbing comfortably over her fingers.

"So, Duke, tell us all about this new clinic of yours. Tell us about the location, we're dying to know."

"It's great, on a nice street; I'll have my apartment above it."

"And here I thought Texas was all ranches." Sass spilled from Iris' lips.

"You've been to Texas a dozen times." James looked at her, "You know that's not true."

"Wait, how often have you gone to Texas, when were these trips?" Cordelia leaned forward.

"I just went with James a few times; I went with him to a few of his cousins' weddings."

Cordelia squinted her eyes in thought, "You told me you were going on art retreats those weekends."

"I didn't want you thinking something more was going on; I was helping a friend out." She turned back to Duke, "You know I saw this great space in the city, it would've been perfect for an animal clinic, near the bakery actually."

"Iris, you might be right, but my Mother rented that space out in the spring, they've had construction going on in there for the last few weeks." Cordelia went back to her salad.

"Your Mom, she owns the building now?"

"Yeah, she was looking for someone to take that space over for a while; I forget if she said what kind of shop it's going to be." She shrugged, "You'll be in Texas anyway."

Duke smiled, he knew that James and Iris knew about him returning to the city, but it seemed like Cordelia wouldn't pick up any clues given to her.

"Duke, bay window, right now." Iris stood up.

"Iris there isn't a bay window here." He looked confused; please don't let her blow this up right now.

"Then the library, right now." She stormed off before he could answer.

Duke followed, knowing not to challenge her right now. "What is it Iris, this must be important, you used my name."

"Tell her."

"Tell her what?"

"That you're the new tenant in her building. That it's your clinic that is going to be next door to her bakery. That your apartment is going to share a wall with hers." Iris shook her head, "Did you know she ran the bakery, that she lived in that building?"

"No, when I met with Mrs. Watson, she didn't mention it; neither did Mr. Watson or Gage." Duke sat on the couch, "Things with Cordelia are complicated, I'm afraid that if she finds out I'm going to not only be in New York but as close as I am, that she'll push me away. Please, Iris, don't tell her."

Iris sighed, knowing she'd already promised not to say anything, but it was getting more difficult, "I promise."

"Cordelia wants her, and I have to have these few days as something, whatever, if she wants more than friendship from me, she's welcome to it. If she wants anything from me this weekend, she gets it. I sure as hell want more than one weekend with her, but I can see it in her eyes, she's terrified to ask for that much, to believe that much can happen. Besides I am going back to Texas on Monday night, I'm just going to be in New York by Thursday morning."

"Who knows you're moving back to the city?"

"The Watson's, you, James, Gage, and Grandpa."

Iris rubbed her head, "Why can't the two of you ever do anything easily, why is it always so damn complicated."

"Pot, meet kettle, I know something is going on with you and James. From the looks of it, it's just as complicated."

Iris ignored him, "If you hurt Cordelia, I will kill you?"

"Iris, when have I ever hurt her?"

"I guess the goat wasn't really your fault," She sighed, "Just be careful with her."

"I will, I promise. Iris, I love her, I never stopped loving her. I've spent the last eight years making sure I could come back to New York with a good career and a hope to win her back. I will give Cordelia anything I can in this lifetime."

"I believe you." Iris opened the door, "Okay Duke, we've cleared that up."

"Iris," Cordelia looked at her friend as they returned, "What did you say to him?"

"Nothing Cinnamon, it's okay."

Cordelia grew silent for the rest of the meal, hoping that Iris hadn't just told Duke her same time next year idea, she wasn't even sure she would ask him about it, she still had time to think, to find out if the next few days would be enough of Duke Shaw to last her a lifetime.

♥

After cleaning up from lunch Cordelia started to make her modeling chocolate, she was thankful that her Mother had texted to let her know she'd grabbed the airbrush supplies sitting on her desk and had them in her bag to bring with her tomorrow.

The kitchen was quiet as she started to make several batches of the modeling chocolate. She was startled when she heard the radio turn on; she looked around slowly and saw Duke on the other side grabbing some things from the cabinet.

"Sorry to disturb you but I've got to get this sauce and marinade made."

"It's fine, I'm almost done, and I realized I can't make these flowers until the morning." She looked up, watching the way he moved, "Did you ever help with the cutting of the modeling chocolate by chance?"

"I sure did, I will assist you in any way that I can Chef Watson."

Cordelia smiled, "No one ever calls me that."

"Well you are one, aren't you?"

"Well yeah, but everyone just calls me Cordelia." She shrugged, "I guess I don't think about the title much, more just the world and how good it feels. I love the way a bride lights up when she sees her wedding cake. I did this great one a few months ago, here let me show you."

Duke moved closer to see the picture on her phone, he was blown away. "Did you make all those flowers yourself?"

"Yeah, it took hours, but it was worth it. Oh, look at this one."

Another amazing cake looked like several travel trunks stacked together, "That's amazing."

"They were travel writers, they fell in love in Paris, he proposed in Venice, they were honeymooning in Fiji, and they'd traveled all over the world together, this was their anniversary cake."

Duke nodded, "Did you ever, you know, go to Paris?"

Cordelia shook her head, "Not yet, I'm saving up. Don't tell Iris, but I was thinking of going this fall, it's not the peak season, but it should still be beautiful. I should have enough put away by then."

"Your secret is safe with me, all your secrets, all your hopes, dreams, everything Cordelia." He looked around to make sure he didn't see James or Iris before he kissed her.

Cordelia pulled away after being lost in the moment, "You know, I might have some time to kill, do you want to go for a walk on the beach with me?"

"That sounds great, but I have a better idea." He went to the fridge, taking out a bottle of white wine he'd gotten earlier, he quickly uncorked it and then corked it again, he grabbed two wine glasses, "We are going to go, watch the ocean and have a drink."

"I like that idea." She took his hand leading him out onto the deck and down the stairs, grabbing the blanket they'd used earlier on the way.

"So, what did you find out earlier?" Cordelia asked as she started collecting shells along the way.

"Apparently they hooked up a couple of times in college, I think more is still going on, I think neither wants to talk about it though." He sighed as they kept in step together. "Iris is afraid I'm going to hurt you."

"Shouldn't you be afraid of me thinking you're dating another goat?"

"That's what I told her." He smiled as they found the perfect spot to sit and enjoy the ocean.

Cordelia helped him with the blanket before the settled down, her body leaning into his. "You know, I don't know why I didn't think you would be here. Rationally I knew you all were still friends. They just try not to talk about you around me. I think I was afraid to hope to see you again. I didn't know how I would react when I saw you, and God forbid if you had someone with you."

"Cordelia, you don't have to do this."

"I know, but you should know, I am so very happy that we have this time. I know it's not much, but I know that I couldn't forgive myself if we didn't have it. I would hate to wake up on the last day of my life and regret not making love to you last night, or this morning, or any other time we do this week. I don't want to regret not dancing with you in the kitchen."

"As you wish, whatever you want from me this week is yours." He kissed her forehead; she was so happy; he couldn't tell her he was moving back; she would just get mad at him.

Cordelia relaxed into him, feeling his arms wrap around her, "Can you believe that Gage is the first one of us to get married?"

"No, I always thought it would be us." His honesty surprised her.

"You thought about us getting married?"

"Of course, I did." He kissed the back of her neck, "I thought about how to ask your Dad and Mom for their blessing, I thought of how to ask Steve and of course Iris as well."

"Really, I never knew that."

"Yeah, I kind of knew how I might propose." He confessed.

Cordelia felt her breath catch, "You did?"

"Yeah, we'd both be home, back in New York, I would take you up to your roof, and it would be beautiful with flowers and lights, we would dance to our song, I would get down on one knee and ask you to be my wife, give you a beautiful ring the moment you said yes."

"Oh, you're so sure I would've said yes, huh?"

"I know you would've." He brushed her hair away from her neck, planting a quick kiss.

"Duke," She gasped, "You're right."

She turned to him, getting lost in his peridot eyes, God she prayed this week would be enough for her.

Before she could kiss him, something came between them, something wet and furry.

Duke took the animal in his arms, "Hey buddy, who are you here with?" He checked and saw no collar, noticing how long the dog's fur was. No one was chasing after him as far as Duke could see.

"Do you think he's a stray?"

"Not sure, he might've just run off." He looked at the dog, "Scottie are you looking for a family, or did you just get excited chasing something and got lost?"

"Scottie?"

"Well, he's a Scottish Terrier." Duke continued to examine the dog, "You need to get cleaned up, and we need to see if we can find who you belong with."

Cordelia couldn't help but smile as she watched him.

Duke caught her, "What?"

"It's just nice; weird seeing you do what you do."

"I know the feeling." He winked at her as he lifted the dog into his arms, "Would you help carry some of this stuff on the way back."

"No problem." She grabbed the half-empty wine bottle and the now empty glasses as Duke wrapped the blanket around the dog, "So, what do we do with Mr. Scottie now?"

"Well, we'll clean him up, see if anyone reported him missing, I'll give him a closer look, make sure he's okay. Someone must be missing him."

"I hope you're housetrained Mr. Scottie; Mrs. Keller would not like it if you peed all over her white carpet the day before everyone arrived for her son's wedding." Cordelia teased him as she and Duke walked back to the house.

When they arrived, he took Scottie upstairs to their bathroom and Cordelia put the wine away and rinsed their glasses before going up to help him. "Do you have everything you need?"

"Yeah, I always carry a few things with me. You never know when you'll need to clean up a lost dog." He'd already filled the tub with water and was easing Scottie in.

The woman that eventually would marry Duke Shaw would be the luckiest in the world, she thought, who else would carry supplies to bathe a dog just in case? And then Cordelia realized that woman wouldn't be her.

She stayed back for a moment, watching him talk to the dog as he shampooed him, she knew she would need a week with him every year, it was the only way. She had to have Duke Shaw in her life, if even for a week at a time.

"Cordelia, could you help with rinsing him off?"

"Yeah, of course," She joined him, she felt better now; her mind was made up.

"Just hold him, yeah like that." He turned the water on, filling a pitcher he found under the sink full so he could rinse Scottie off.

"I think Mrs. Keller will be okay if we keep the dog up here, but we're going to have to take him out, won't we?"

"Yeah, I texted James and asked him to pick up a collar, leash, and some food for this little guy."

"That's good." Cordelia looked at Scottie, "What if no one is missing him?"

"We'll figure that out when the time comes." He poured another pitcher of water over the dog, "Cordelia grab those towels, we're going to have a wet dog to try and dry."

She grabbed the first two she could find, dropping one near Duke as she made sure hers was unfolded, just in time as Scottie began to shake himself dry.

Duke grabbed the towel and tried to get a hold of Scottie, Cordelia following his lead as they tried to dry off the dog.

"Cordelia, Duke?" Iris called out from the bedroom door.

"We're in here, drying the dog," Cordelia called out and a moment later Iris and James were in the doorway.

"We got the stuff you asked for, I called Gage he said just don't let the dog downstairs, keep him up here, take him out when needed and should be fine. Any mess, the damage is on you guys." James put the bag down on the counter.

Iris watched, "Look here you two." She pulled her phone up and snapped a picture of Cordelia and Duke drying the dog. "Great, now get me one of just the dog so we can tweet out that he got found."

"Oh, great idea, send me a copy of the picture and I'll post it to my Instagram."

"Yeah, same I'll post it on Facebook."

They got a quick picture of Scottie, and a moment later Cordelia and Duke' phones buzzed with the pictures sent to them, "Thought you two might like a copy of the first one as well."

"Thanks, Iris." Cordelia was already uploading to Instagram as Duke attached a collar to Scottie.

❤

@IrisLaArt
If anyone recognizes this adorable little guy who was found in Coral Shore this afternoon, please tweet me #ScottieDog
@IrisLaArt
How adorable are these two with the dog they found on the beach this afternoon? #CordukeReunion
❤

James was quiet as he retweeted both of Iris's tweets while he watched his friends, it was going to be a long, long night.

"So, we should probably get dinner going." Duke looked up at his friends and then down at Scottie, "You be a good boy and stay in here, Cordelia and I will come back to check on you later."

"Wow, Duke really is a Veterinarian huh; weird to see him in action."

"I'm right here."

"I know." Iris looked over at Cordelia, "Hey we should go run and get some stuff for tomorrow since I know you'll be busy with the chocolate flowers most of the day."

"Good idea, you guys don't mind, do you?"

"No, of course not; we'll have dinner ready when you get back." Duke wanted to kiss Cordelia goodbye, but he knew he couldn't.

"You know what we should make to go with dinner?" James walked towards the door to Duke' room, "Sangria, we should make some Sangria, the girls love it." He glanced towards Duke' bed again still bothered that it didn't appear slept in.

Duke saw an odd look on James's face, "What's wrong?"

"Either you're really good at duplicating how the bed was made when we got here, or you didn't sleep in here last night."

"I fell asleep on the chair." He lied.

"Whatever you say, man, whatever you say."

Duke made a mental note to make sure both his and Cordelia's beds looked slept in by the morning, even if they didn't sleep.

♥

"So, let me get this straight, he's gotten to see you bake and you got to see him rescue a dog?" Iris asked from the driver's seat as they drove to the market.

"Yeah, crazy huh, it was weird to see him in action; he really did it, Iris, just like I knew he would."

"Cor, if just a big if-if Duke were to tell you he was moving back to New York, would you be willing to try again with him?"

Cordelia looked out the window, "I don't know, I would probably be scared. Here, now, I know that Monday anything that might happen will be over."

"But what if it's not?"

"Iris, he has a place for his clinic all lined up, he's been working the last eight years towards this future, I messed up and any plans we had are gone. He lives in Texas now; decisions have already been made."

She got it now; Cordelia was terrified that another misunderstanding would tear them apart. "Has anything happened between you and Duke so far?"

"We kissed." Cordelia spoke dreamily, "Iris, it was better than I remembered. He's stronger now, but still gentle."

Iris parked the car, should she tell her? No, it would just make her angry and she would ruin whatever she had going on with Duke. No, she would keep his secret for now, besides Cordelia wasn't letting him tell her, maybe deep down she already understood and was too afraid to admit it. "So, what do we need for this movie night?"

"Popcorn, copies of the movies she wanted, what were they again?"

Iris pulled up on her phone, "The Princess Bride, Magic Mike XXL, and When Harry Met Sally."

Cordelia nodded, "I think we can track those down, let's get shopping!"

While they gathered the items, they needed for the mini-bachelorette party Iris forgot to worry about Cordelia until she saw the box of condoms she tossed into the car. "Cor?"

"What?"

"What do you need those for?"

"Just in case, better to be prepared, don't you think?"

"Yeah . . . I guess."

"Iris, Duke and I are not going to sneak down to the beach and make love during sunrise."

Iris didn't say anything, something about the way Cordelia spoke kept her quiet, "So can you believe those movie choices?"

"Yeah, actually I can." Cordelia got dreamy, "I mean two of the most romantic movies of all time, and then one of the most pro-female movies of all time. Besides, you know I'm a sucker for The Princess Bride."

Iris's phone vibrated and she quickly checked it before slipping it back in her pocket.

"Was that a dirty message from oh I don't know, James?"

"No, just people re-tweeting the lost dog picture."

"Oh, I know what we need!" Cordelia raced off to the health and beauty aisle and Iris followed, finding her with an arm full of face masks.

"I don't know if she'll be down for that?"

"She will be if we are. Come on." Cordelia tossed them in the cart before pulling it to the next aisle, stopping before a display of dog toys.

"Oh man, you're going to end up with the dog."

Cordelia shook her head as she picked up a squeeze toy that looked like a hotdog, "We'll find his owner, probably before everyone arrives. Besides, what makes you think I'd be the one to end up with Scottie?"

"Just a feeling, you know with Duke going back to Texas on Monday night." Iris breathed out.

"Well, we'll come to that decision if we have to."

"So, we need anything else? Do you need anything else?"

"Just some more powdered sugar and butter, I've got to get the cakes frosted tonight."

Iris followed Cordelia around the store, she feared Monday night, Cordelia would be a mess and how many days after that before Duke was back in New York, and how long would it take for Cordelia to see him again. Would he rush to her door first thing, or would he wait to see how long it took her to notice Dr. Shaw painted on the clinic door?

CHAPTER 5

As Cordelia put away the items, they got for the party she made sure she put the box of condoms in her jacket, just in case.

Duke and James came in with the food from the grill, they'd made chicken, corn on the cob, macaroni salad, and the girl's favorite Sangria sat on the table waiting for them.

Iris came in, "Hey James, come here."

"Why, we're about to eat."

"Now!" Iris was tense as she pulled James into the library.

"That was weird, right?" Duke looked towards the hall, wondering what that was all about.

"Very, but maybe she realized they need to talk."

"Maybe, come here." He pulled her into his arms, "I missed you."

"I missed you too, how's Scottie."

"He's okay, I found a stud finder, but he's not chipped."

"Really?"

"Yeah, and I called around no one's reported him missing." He shrugged, not really understanding it himself.

"That's such a shame." Cordelia took the moment to breathe in his scent.

"At least he found us." Duke pushed the hair from her eyes.

"So, I have to frost those cakes tonight, but after that, I'm all yours until dawn."

"What happens at dawn?" He flashed her a smile.

"That's when you become my assistant and we get to work on the chocolate flowers for the cake."

He kissed her forehead, "As you wish," then started to nibble her ear when they heard the Library door open.

"Everything okay?"

"Yeah, it's fine." Iris put her phone down on the counter.

"Anyone tweet you about Scottie?"

"No, just retweets, sorry guys, you might have to fight for custody." Iris shrugged before going and pouring herself a glass of Sangria.

"You sure you're okay?"

"Yeah, let's eat." ❤

After dinner, James and Iris disappeared up to her room, "Well if they didn't think something was going on already, they will now."

"I have like a thousand new followers James; this is blowing up. What if someone from NYCBuzz.com curates the tweets?"

"Then Cordelia and Duke get to see that we want them back together and to stop being idiots." James didn't know what they could do to stop the influx of interest on their friends. "We either stop tweeting or keep going and just let it be what it is."

"Either way they'll kill us. I wonder how Texas, Duke he can be." Iris tried to joke but she was a bit worried.

James sighed, "We just have to hope that no one mentions it to them. Besides no one has curated them yet that we know of. When Duke is officially in the city, they're together, then we tell them."

"We might have to tell them something else to calm them down or at least distract them."

"They'll probably be mad about that as well."

"Let them." Iris sighed, "We have to turn off our notifications, they can't know our phones are going off like crazy."

"Good idea, we won't check until we're back at home at the loft on Monday night."

"So, this is like a performance art piece, we're telling their love story because they're too damn stubborn to do it themselves."

James nodded, "Exactly Sugar, most people are rooting for them. I mean Cheese Soufflé is probably the only one not."

"We started this; we have to finish it." Iris put her phone down. "Now we need to figure out something so that we get them talking tonight, being honest with each other."

"Like this?" James pulled an app up on his phone.

Iris smiled, "Perfect!"

♥

@IrisLaArt
Gotta hand it to @JamesSheath, he found the perfect game to get Cordelia and Duke to play tonight. #TheGameofTruth #CordukeReunion

@GKNYC
I was going to text you and tell you guys to download that! @IrisLaArt @JamesSheath #CordukeReunion

@TheGameofTruth
@IrisLaArt Hope it gets your couple together! We're rooting for them #CordukeReunion

♥

"Okay you two, grab the s'mores fixings and meet us out on the deck in five minutes," James called out to Duke and Cordelia who had just brought Scottie back from a walk.

"What's going on?" Duke called out.

James waved his phone, "We're going to play a game. Don't forget the rest of the Sangria and the beers."

Duke turned to Cordelia, "What game do you think it will be, Never Have I Ever or Truth or Dare?"

"Truth or Dare I'm sure." She grabbed a snack tray from one of the cabinets and filled it with the stuff for s'mores; Duke meanwhile was gathering the Sangria, beers, and glasses.

On the deck, James and Iris had gotten the fire pit going and had set the chairs up around it. Iris helped Cordelia set everything up on the table while Duke helped James light the torches to keep the bugs away.

"Okay, so what game are we going to play?" Cordelia sat back in her favorite chair with a small glass of Sangria; she still had work to do later that night after all.

"The Game of Truth, Gage sent me the link earlier." James explained, "This app will give us random questions and we'll have to answer them truthfully."

"You guys needed an app for Truth or Dare?" Cordelia raised an eyebrow at her friends.

"No dares, we're not in high school anymore. I mean the kissing combinations here have already happened. I don't think we need that." Iris explained as she pulled a piece of fruit from her drink.

"Well let's do this." Duke sat in the seat between Cordelia and James. "Who's first?"

"Duke, you're first." James tapped the screen and a question came up, "What is your most embarrassing picture?"

He had to think for a moment, "I guess I would have to say the one that broke me and Cordelia up."

She blushed when she heard his answer, "Oh come on Duke, you were in a Frat for how long, I'm sure something more embarrassing came up."

"Nope, I'm never living that picture down and if my brothers ever find out, I'm really never living that one down." He took a sip of his beer.

James nodded, "Okay, Butterscotch," He tapped for a new question, "What lie have you told that hurt someone?"

She knew the answer, they all knew, it still made her blood feel cold as she looked to Duke, "That I didn't love Duke, I hurt a lot of people with that."

He reached for her hand giving it a gentle squeeze to let her know it was okay.

"Okay, Iris." James turned to the blonde, smiling automatically as he looked into her blue eyes before tapping for a new question, "What was the worst encounter you had with a police officer?"

Iris covered her hands with her face, "Oh geez, okay, Junior Year, after the Contessa Jovi show, I accidentally spilled this bottle of red paint all over an officer. I don't even remember why I had a bottle of paint with me, but it ended up all over Officer Bo Arthur of the NYPD."

"That was more of meet cute; you dated that guy for like three months." James reminded her, a flare of jealousy in his voice.

"It was still my worst encounter with a police officer."

"You dated a cop, you never told me that." Cordelia looked over at her best friend, sure earlier she'd admitted they weren't as close as they once had been, but how much else did she not know?

Iris shrugged, "It wasn't that serious; besides he was really in love with this lawyer lady that he married a few years ago."

"Okay James, your turn, let me get you a question." Duke held his hand out for the phone which James placed in his hand. "Okay, tell us about your most awkward date."

James laughed before locking eyes with Iris, "Well the girl didn't realize it was a date until about halfway through dinner, and then she bolted, told me her best friend called and needed her. Only thing was I knew her best friend wasn't in town, wasn't even in the state. But at least I didn't end up with a smoothie poured over me."

Duke and Cordelia watched the way James kept his eyes on Iris while he spoke; maybe things weren't what they suspected after all.

"Who's next? Duke, ask Cordelia the next question." James suggested when he realized they were watching him closely.

Duke tapped the screen, "Oh boy, why did you break up with your last boyfriend?"

Cordelia couldn't believe it that app probably had thousands of questions and that's the one she got, "Every boyfriend I've had besides you Duke, I've broken up with because I was still in love with someone else."

Duke was smiling like an idiot with that answer before he looked to Iris before tapping the screen for the next question, "Iris, what was the most awkward romantic encounter you have had?"

Iris visibly became stiff as she looked around at her friends, "Freshmen year of college, Valentine's Night, I tried to throw myself at Blake, only to find him with his girlfriend. I was heartbroken, that night I called up one of my guy friends, he came over, and I lost my virginity to him."

Duke looked to James; getting the impression that James hadn't known Iris was a virgin that night.

"I'm sorry that Blake was never smart enough to see how amazing you are." Cordelia broke the silence, "And in case you're wondering that girlfriend was a bitch and a half. Uncle Casper had to have his security detail remove her from a family party."

Iris smiled, "Thanks, but I think in the end things worked out how they should've."

"Another question for James," Duke tapped the screen again, "Who is the person you most regret kissing?"

James closed his eyes, "Nicole, in tenth grade. She was only using me to make Wade jealous. Cordelia, your turn to ask the questions."

"Okay then," Cordelia took the phone from Duke and tapped the screen, "What is your favorite Christmas Eve tradition?"

"It does not say that, does it?" Duke looked at the screen and it did, "Okay, you might think this is weird, and I hope to God you don't think it's creepy. Iris and James only know I did this once, but I did this every year when I come home for the holiday. I've spent the last eight Christmas Eves, sitting on your fire escape, trying to get the nerve to talk to you. I never get close enough to the window that you can see me, but I've seen you and God that sounds beyond creepy."

"And yet still better than Cheese Soufflé!" Iris was shocked she could still do that voice after all these years.

"You've really come to try and talk to me every Christmas Eve?" Cordelia couldn't help but laugh, "Every New Year's Eve, I waited on the roof hoping you would show up."

"I always went back to Texas on New Year's Eve."

"Okay, Iris," Cordelia looked to her friend as she pulled up the next question, "your turn, what is your dream wedding?"

"A spring afternoon, just me and my fiancé, a bouquet of flowers picked up earlier that day. We would wear our best outfits, exchange vows in front of a Justice of the Peace at the courthouse. Afterward dinner at our favorite restaurant, and then a night in the Plaza for a honeymoon." Something about the way Iris spoke reminded Cordelia more of memory than a dream.

"That sounds really nice, but what about friends and family?" Cordelia asked, suddenly wondering if Iris was keeping a major secret from her.

"It was my dream wedding Cor, come on now. Ask James the next question." Iris wanted the attention off her.

Cordelia pulled the next one up, "Okay then, James, what did you do the first night of your freshmen year of college?"

"Easy, I helped Iris set up her bed in her dorm. We went and got some cinder blocks, so it was sort of lofted, her roommate had taken up the majority of the storage space we had to create some. So, the first night of college I was helping the blonde beauty."

"You guys really did bond in college didn't you?" Duke watched them over the fire flames.

"It was the first night, you guys were already long gone, who was I going to call Mark?"

"Oh, come on, you know he would've done it for some corn chips." Duke teased.

"Shut up Duke, Cordelia give me the phone, it's my turn to ask."

"Here you go." Cordelia handed the phone off, nervous of what question would come up next.

"Oh, this is a good one." Iris had a mischievous grin on her face, "Okay Duke, what is the longest you've gone without sex?"

Duke thought for a moment, "Seven years, ten months, give or take a few days."

"You're kidding me, really?" Iris was surprised and then she started to add up that time, "So wait, is Cordelia the only girl you've ever been with?"

"Iris!" Cordelia was red herself having figured out exactly when he'd meant as the last time, well before last night.

Duke smiled, "It's true, Cordelia, you're the only woman I've ever had sex with, of course, it's always been more than that between us, we made love."

Cordelia tried not to smile, "That's the sweetest thing I think I've ever heard."

"I'm glad you think so." Duke took a sip of his beer, "Iris, ask Cordelia the next question."

"Okay," Iris tapped the phone, "Oh this is easy we all know the answer to this one. Cor, do you have a tattoo?"

"You're all so sure of yourselves, on this one huh? You all think you know the answer don't you." Cordelia put her drink down and looked around at her friends, "I do have a tattoo."

"What?" All three of them were shocked.

"Where?" Duke' was shocked, but he knew it must be small if he hadn't seen it yet.

"When?" Iris was trying to process how her friend had never told her this.

"Why?" James just couldn't believe his little Butterscotch had gotten inked.

"It's tiny, like the size of a dime. It's my Greek letters in a spot that very few people will ever see, and it's a pale color so unless you were looking for it, you wouldn't notice it. I got it gosh Junior year of college during Spring Break in Las Vegas, at this place just off the strip." She looked to Duke, "You know I think some Frat guys from your school were there then, actually they were ZGNs."

"No, this is getting better, come on Duke, tell me you got inked to."

"It's small." He confessed, "My Mama would kill me if she knew. It's hidden, most of my brothers were getting massive ones on their arms and chests and I was like let's go for one the size of a dime."

"Wait, Iris, do you think these two might have been at the same place, the same time, in Las Vegas?" James moved closer to her as they looked at the former couple.

Iris nodded, "You know, if I remember correctly, they did both go to Las Vegas the same week that year."

Cordelia and Duke looked over at each other, "Do you think it's possible?" He finally asked.

"Oh, come on, I'm sure lots of Frat guys and Sorority girls went and got tattoos in Las Vegas."

"You know, I think they went to Tahoe the same week once as well." James reminded Iris.

"Oh yeah." She nodded with a smile, "And didn't they both go to Mardi Gras the same year in New Orleans?"

"That they did." James and Iris turned back to Cordelia and Duke, "Interesting, don't you think?"

"Oh, come on guys, you really think that Duke and I were in the same place, at the same time, multiple times over the years and never saw each other?"

"It's possible, or maybe you did and told yourselves you were seeing things." Iris rose from her seat to get a refill, "Maybe fate was trying to put you two together."

"Are you two done playing matchmaker for the evening?" Duke rose from his seat.

"That's not what we're doing, swear." Iris smiled; the Sangria having gotten to her.

Cordelia rolled her eyes, "We should take Scottie for one last walk, and let these two do whatever they're doing."

"Good idea." Duke looked to his friends again, "Seriously, no need to play matchmaker, it'll happen when it happens."

"Sure Duke, sure!" Iris called out as she sat down on James's lap.

"Iris, no more Sangria," James warned.

"But you make it the best, how can I not want it?"

"Come here, let's go to bed."

"We have to tweet first."

"What do you want to tweet?"

"Lots of things." Iris took out her phone and started, James knew he couldn't stop her.

❤

@IrisLaArt
How sweet, Cordelia and Duke have only been with each other. #TotesAdorbs #CordukeReunion
@IrisLaArt
Cordelia and Duke both have "dime sized" tattoos of their Greek letters; they probably got about the same night in Las Vegas. #CordukeReunion
@IrisLaArt
Duke says #TheGoat picture is his most embarrassing and he will never live it down. Hell yeah, he won't. #CordukeReunion
@IrisLaArt
Duke climbed up Cordelia's fire escape every year to try and talk to her on Christmas Eve, always chickened out. #CordukeReunion
@IrisLaArt
Cordelia admitted that she broke up w/ every bf because she still loves Duke. Take that Cheese Soufflé! #CordukeReunion
@IrisLaArt
Duke and Cordelia never knew they both went to Tahoe or New Orleans the same time either. Wonder how close they came to #CordukeReunion then.
@GKNYC
I'm guessing @JamesSheath made Sangria for you @IrisLaArt and Cordelia?
@JamesSheath
I told her not to tweet, but she didn't listen to me. @GKNYC
@GKNYC
So, anything to report you 2 saw not from the game? #CordukeReunion @JamesSheath
@JamesSheath
Not really @IrisLaArt spilled everything already. #CordukeReunion

❤

Cordelia followed Duke as Scottie did most of the leading down the beach, for a small dog he had a lot of energy and he knew where he wanted to take them on the final walk of the evening. A day ago, she was burning mad at Duke, having carried it around for eight ridiculous years, and now they'd made love several times, would make love again tonight. It was inevitable.

"This air, this smell, I miss it most of the year when I'm back in the city," Cordelia announced as she caught up to him.

"I know what you mean; I've missed it when I'm in Texas." Duke picked up after Scottie with a plastic baggie be brought with him, "How often do you girls get up here these days?"

"Not often enough, Iris could probably spend as much time up here as she wanted, except she has her gallery show in a few weeks. I usually spend a week, with some weekends and of course the Fourth of July holiday. But I do miss when we were all still in high school and we could spend all the summer vacation here. Do you remember when Iris worked for the daycare program as the art counselor?"

"She was miserable, James and I were teaching baseball and basketball, Gage was teaching computer stuff, and you got the little kids." He thought back to that summer, it was one of his favorites, it was the second one they'd spent out here; they were sixteen, "I also remember you and me sneaking out to walk on the beach in the moonlight."

"We barely had parental supervision; we had no one to sneak away from."

"Well Gage, Iris, James, we snuck away from them." Duke turned to her as Scottie splashed in the waves not far from them, "Kind of like we are now."

Cordelia blushed, "Maybe in some way some things never change."

"So, do you want company while you frost the cakes, or do you want me to go find something to do on my lonesome?"

Cordelia turned away from him; she loved having him in the kitchen with her. He was the only one she wasn't desperate to throw out, "I think you should find something to occupy your time. You'll distract me, and I won't get it done. Besides, the quicker I get it done, the sooner we can find a way to pass the early morning hours just the two of us."

"As you wish," Duke kissed her cheek from the side before whistling for Scottie who came running towards him.

"What are you going to call your clinic, Shaw Animal Hospital?" Cordelia felt his arms around her as they started to walk back towards the house.

"Um, you know I have something in mind, I'm just waiting to make sure it's not already taken." He smiled to himself, as he held her as close as he could. He never wanted to let her go.

Once back at the house Duke took Scottie back upstairs and got him settled in Cordelia's room. He then looked around his own, which he hadn't spent much time in yet, but tonight he would take Cordelia to bed, his bed.

He searched around the room finding a few sets of flameless candles, one thing about the Keller men; they always tried to be prepared for romance. He went out into the hallway, grabbing a couple of the white roses that had been displayed before they arrived, he tore the petals off, sprinkling them on the bed.

He stood back, looking around at his handiwork, this was perfect, she was going to love it.

"Duke!" Cordelia's voice startled him, and he realized it was coming from the intercom.

"Yes?" He pressed the button down wondering what was wrong.

"Could you come to the kitchen, I need some help."

"I'll be right down." He smiled, wondering what she needed him for.

Duke found Cordelia standing before a five-layer cake that had a perfect layer of buttercream frosting on it. "Wow."

"I can't lift it myself, could you help me bring it into the walk in?"

"Of course." He went to the other side of the cake, "Just tell me when to lift."

"Now." They both picked it up, slowly moving towards the walk in and setting it down on the car she'd placed inside for it.

It took a moment before Cordelia seemed to breathe again, "Thank you."

"Anything for you, it looks great already." He wrapped his arms around her from behind, feeling her sink against him.

"You know I've made hundreds of cakes, but this one has me the most nervous, I don't know why."

Duke kissed the back of her neck, "Because it's for your friends, this one is personal, it means more."

"So, what should we do now?"

"Come with me Cordelia, I have something set up for you."

"You did?" She couldn't imagine what as they went up the back set of stairs, he pushed open the door of his room revealing the candles and rose petals on the bed, "Oh Duke."

He watched the way her face lit up with surprise as she walked into the room and he closed the door behind himself, "I thought tonight should be special, I fear tomorrow night we might not get to spend as much time together."

Her eyes welled with tears, what man did stuff like this; Duke Shaw, that's who.

He turned on the playlist from his phone, "Over the years, I've looked at this playlist and thought about deleting it." He told her as he sat in front of her, reaching for the buttons on her shirt, "But something always stops me. All the playlists I ever made for you are still synced up on my iTunes, collecting digital dust."

"Is this from prom night, the night we lost our virginities?" She heard the familiar love songs she hadn't let herself listen to in years.

He pushed her shirt off her shoulders, letting it fall to the ground as he pulled her close, kissing her flat stomach, "One and the same."

"Duke?"

"Shh, let me take this slow Cordelia." He looked up into her brown eyes, golden with the candlelight, the ones that were always looking at him in his dreams.

He saw her locket hanging from its thin chain, his fingers picking it up, opening it, a smile meeting his eyes, "You always wear this?" He remembered when they took the pictures looking back at him.

"Always, I haven't opened it in a long time, but I always wear it. I've never been able to take it off."

"So, I'm always near your heart." He placed his hand over her heart as he spoke.

Cordelia blushed, "I guess you have been."

Duke rose from the bed before capturing her mouth with his, his hands on her back and after a moment her clasp undone, and she was shedding her bra. Duke broke the kiss long enough to peel off his t-shirt before he and Cordelia fell on the bed.

"I want to memorize every inch of you." He told her as he worked to remove her pants.

"Ditto." She felt his hands on her bare legs as he pulled away her panties, and she was pretty sure this is what heaven felt like, being touched by Duke.

Duke pulled away to strip out of his jeans and boxers, his eyes on Cordelia as she watched him. He needed to see that look from her for the rest of his life.

They lay on the bed, fingers exploring once familiar bodies that had changed over eight years, harder muscles, new scars.

Duke rolled Cordelia onto her stomach as he kissed her back, stopping when he saw the pale pink Greek letters, "Oh come on, you're kidding me." His fingers traced each small letter.

"What, I told you all about this earlier; you are the first person outside of the Gamma's to see it."

"Look." Duke positioned himself next to Cordelia so she could look, and that's when she saw his own tattoo, about the same size as hers, in about the same spot on his body.

Cordelia traced the letters with her fingers, "What do you think would've happened if we'd run into each other."

"I can't think of that Cordelia, knowing now that you were so close, we were so close."

She smiled before kissing him, rolling him onto his back before taking control of their lovemaking.

She reached for a condom from the nightstand, tearing the package open, time was fleeting, she could feel it now, she needed Duke and needed as much of him as possible. She guided him into her.

Cordelia and Duke moved slowly together, each trying to memorize the sensations and feelings.

Duke held Cordelia against his hard body as they sat up, still connected.

Slivers of moonlight mixed with the glow of the electric candles, washing over their bodies as they took their time with each other.

Cordelia tried not to let her declarations of love escape from her, he couldn't know, he couldn't understand how important this was for her. She cried out his name just before his mouth crashed down on hers, his fingers tangled in her hair as pure bliss took over them both.

Her body was limp as he held onto her, planting soft kisses on her neck.

"Do you know how beautiful you are?" His fingers splayed her face before he kissed her, not giving her the chance to argue with him.

"Duke," she broke the kiss, "Do you think their might have been other moments where we've been in the same place, same time, you know besides what James and Iris mentioned?"

"First weekend of Coachella senior year?"

She nodded, "Gamma Convention, Junior year in Orlando?"

"Yup," His fingers ran along her back, "Durango, Thanksgiving week, Senior year."

"Yeah, we went skiing at Purgatory." She looked at him, lost in the way he gazed over her body. "How did we not see each other?"

"Too many people pulling in different directions, or a guiding hand knew we weren't ready to see each other yet."

"And it just takes Gage getting married for us to finally see each other."

"Well, that and you falling into my arms on the train." He pushed the hair from her eyes, "This time with you is more than I ever dreamed possible."

"Duke, you don't have to say that."

"I know, I want to say it, Cordelia, you are the first woman I ever loved, the only one."

Cordelia didn't think as she reached for the locket still hanging around her neck, "I don't think you'll ever know how important you are to me, how important this time together is."

"Do you know how happy I am you're giving me any kind of shot? When I'm with you I'm on cloud nine." He searched her eyes, "For eight years I wondered what happened, for eight years I've wondered what it would be like to really see you again. I've been terrified, nervous, hopeful, every time I came back to New York or up to Coral Shore."

"You will never know how sorry I am about how things ended. I think maybe it was difficult to believe in myself, us when you were surrounded by beautiful Texas girls and apparently goats. Why would you want me?"

"Cordelia, you are the sun to my moon, one of the most caring people I know, you make me calm, and life without you just isn't as sweet. Your smile, makes me smile; watching you get excited about something, passionate about it, affects me like no one else."

"Let's not talk anymore." Cordelia kissed him, pulling him onto the bed with her.

His hands caressed her body; he knew he had to be careful, he'd almost told her that he loved her. She would go running from him if he confessed, he couldn't let that happen.

They shared lazy kisses, rolling in his bed before making love again, more urgency this time leading to Cordelia shuddering under his body and he called out her name repeatedly. They slept for a little while until the alarm on her phone went off. They showed together, quickly dressed before they took Scottie for a quick walk and returned to the kitchen to make the chocolate flowers for the cake.

"Time to put those muscles to the test," She told him as she coated the top of the counter with powdered sugar, "You get to roll out the chocolate."

"How thick?"

"As thick as a dime." She handed him a rolling pin and the modeling chocolate.

"As you wish." He watched her as she got out her other supplies and set up for the actual work. When he was done rolling and Cordelia was happy with how thick the sheet was she handed him a small circular cookie cutter and directed him to cut as many as possible.

She worked to create the petals, Duke watched her, the way she took her fingers and was able to create something so realistic from chocolate and corn syrup, it was amazing.

"This must be boring for you; I won't blame you if you go back to bed or take Scottie out again."

"This isn't boring at all Cordelia; I love watching you work. You look so at peace and watching the way you turn these boring little circles into chocolate flowers is amazing."

Cordelia could feel the blush on her cheeks, "You are too kind Duke."

"Is there anything else I could do to help you?"

Cordelia looked at the clock, "Actually if you go in my work bag, you'll find a recipe for some muffins; maybe you could put the batter together while I finish these up."

"Anything at all for you Princess." Duke was realizing that the more time they spent together the harder was going to be when he went back to Texas and Cordelia thought he would be gone forever.

For several moments the kitchen was silent as Cordelia worked and Duke made the muffin batter, every few seconds he would look up at her. If middle school Cordelia could see herself now, she would never believe it.

Cordelia stood up stretching and counting the flowers she had made, she only needed ten, but she had twenty. She picked up the tray that held them and brought them to the walk-in freezer. When she came back Duke was setting the oven to preheat.

They cleaned the kitchen quickly just as it was time to put the muffins in the oven. As they baked Duke turned the radio on, insisting that Cordelia dance with him.

"I think you found the only station that plays slow songs anymore." She felt his fingers tease the back of his neck.

"Do you think your Dad would still freak out if he knew I'd been in your room?"

Cordelia chuckled, "Probably, I miss having a bay window, my apartment doesn't have one. Sometimes when I need to think I go up to my parent's apartment and sit in my old room."

"You should always have a bay window." He thought for a moment, smiling when he remembered his apartment had one.

"Thank you for thinking so."

"Remember when you guys all came down to Texas, and you and Iris set up the little bay window area in Grandpa's living room?"

"Yeah, he promised it would always be there."

"It is, my cousins, they're about ten, they sit there talking all day long."

"Bay windows are magical." She rested her head on his shoulder, letting herself dream about what a life with Duke could be. It wouldn't be exactly like this, but it would still be sweet. If only he were staying in New York if only her mother hadn't rented out that apartment and retail space. The apartment was perfect; it even had a bay window.

"What are you thinking?"

"That as soon as everyone else arrives; we won't get to dance in the kitchen anymore while the muffins are baking."

Duke spun her out before pulling her back to him, "Any chance I get to dance with you, I plan on taking."

The timer for the oven drowned out the stereo; Duke removed the muffins and set them to cool before turning the oven off. He looked outside; sunrise would be soon.

"We should take Scottie out again; he's going to be stuck upstairs more than an active dog like him would like."

"Sounds like a great idea."

They walked slowly down the beach; Cordelia filling her bucket with shells. She placed it at the bottom of the deck steps when they got back to the house. Duke grabbed the blanket, laying it over him and Cordelia as they laid down on the double chaise lounge with Scottie between them. They watched the sunrise and fell asleep.

♥

"Duke?" Iris opened the bedroom door expecting to find her friend or at least the dog in the room, she went through the bathroom and opening

Duke' door, discovering the set-up of candles and the scattered rose petals and an unmade bed.

She hit dial on her phone, "Duke' room, now."

James didn't even have time to disagree before she hung up and he was walking in, "Romantic, right?"

Iris studied the room and saw his laptop open. "Come on Duke, don't have a password." She pushed the mousepad thrilled when the machine woke without having to put in a password.

"What are you looking at?"

"Look at the playlist title."

Prom Night

James didn't get it, "Why would he have a playlist named that, and be playing it last night."

"Honey, he pretty much recreated the night they lost their virginities." She explained, "Cordelia told me all about it yesterday, the candles, the rose petals, the only thing I don't see is the sparkling cider."

"Well if that happened, why are we in this room and they're not?"

"The dog, maybe they took it for a walk." Iris rushed out of the room and down the stairs.

She was surprised she didn't see any sign of Cordelia or Duke, except for a fresh batch of muffins sitting on the counter.

"I think I found them," James called from the deck door.

"Where, on the beach?" Iris looked towards the ocean but saw no one.

"Nope, right there, asleep on the deck." He pointed towards them.

Iris lifted her phone taking a quick picture, "This is good."

♥

@IrisLaArt
They think they're fooling us, come on they're so getting back together. #CordukeReunion

♥

"Should we wake them?" James was ready to open the door.

"Yeah, let's go see them talk their way out of this one."

"Oh Mr. Watson, I don't think you want to go out there!" James called into the air.

Duke popped up, "Not my shoes, please!"

Cordelia sat up, "What's going on?"

"You know, I think that's what we should be asking the two of you." Iris crossed her arms over her chest, "Now spill or I show the picture I took of the two of you just now to Tony when he gets here in a few hours."

"Iris," Cordelia looked at her best friend, "You wouldn't."

"Try me, what's going on?"

"We were watching the sunrise with Scottie, that's all. I guess we fell asleep."

"Library now Cordelia," Iris stormed into the house and Cordelia followed, "I saw his bedroom Cordelia; I know you two have had sex. What are you doing?"

"I'm getting as much of Duke as I can before he goes back to Texas on Monday." She stared at her friend, "I'm getting the sweetest moments from him Iris, and we've slow danced in the kitchen. He's helped me with the baking, he's kissed me, and we've talked. You know there were other trips we missed each other on."

"Like what?"

"Coachella, Orlando, and Durango."

"Cordelia, do you love him?"

"Yes."

Iris nodded, she knew the answer to her next question, "Do you think he loves you still?"

She was silent, she didn't want to answer.

"Cordelia, answer me."

"I think he might still have some feelings for me, but he's leaving on Monday."

"Ask him to stay in New York, ask him to move to New York." Iris encouraged.

"I can't." Cordelia shook her head, "When I sent that promise ring back to him eight years ago, I lost all rights to ask him to build his life in New York. He's spent all that time in Texas, that's longer than he ever lived in New York."

"You act like he never left Texas; he spent a summer working for your mother at the bakery, why would he do that? To be near you, but no that summer you took an internship with your Uncle. And then he comes home every Christmas, every year Cordelia he comes home for his Mother's birthday. He comes up here to Coral Shore every summer with Gage and James."

"Wait, have you all been hanging out with Duke during his Christmas trips, during all these trips and not telling me?"

"Yes," Iris confessed, "And you know what, he asked about you every time. He asked if he should go see you. I'm amazed you never saw him.

Cordelia was silent as she processed this information, "I'm tired; I think I'm going to go to bed."

"Cordelia, don't get upset." Iris kicked the floor realizing she might have just ruined things, and she didn't even tell her that Duke was moving back to New York.

CHAPTER 6

Cordelia raced through the kitchen, out onto the deck and down to the beach.

Duke and James didn't know what could've happened, but Duke didn't want to wait around to find out. He left after her, leaving Scottie with James.

"Cordelia!" He called out as he chased her down the sand, "Cordelia!"

"You come home to New York all the time! You hang out with our friends!"

"Yes." He tried to read her face, but he couldn't tell if she was angry or sad, or what.

She sat in the sand putting her head in her hands, "So you and everyone else just decided that I shouldn't know you still came to New York."

Duke sat next to her, reaching out to tilt her head up to look at him, "I never asked them not to tell you that. I've spent the past almost eight years hoping that you would be at Iris's loft for a party or Gage's brownstone for dinner. I think they thought not throwing us together was better."

"The committee to protect Cordelia really outdid itself this time."

"Yeah, I guess it did, wait does this mean James took my place?"

"I think so." She reached over hugging him, "They know we slept together last night, Iris and James went in your room looking for us."

He sighed, "Does it matter?"

"Not really, except that they'll try to make this more then what it is."

He should tell her; he should tell her right now.

"I told Iris that I lost any right to ask you to change your life and move to New York. You've been building a life for the past eight years, I can't ask you to change that, not after how I ruined things between us. You already have things in motion."

"Cordelia . . ."

"Wait." She stopped him, her fingers on his lips, "I do have a radical idea."

Was Cordelia about to suggest he thought she was?

"I like what we have this week, right now, right here. We don't have the pressure to move on to the next step, we don't have to define this. Isn't that where we always had trouble before?" Her eyes started to glaze with tears, "I like making love with you any chance we get, I like dancing with you in the kitchen, and I think I'm okay with knowing it will all end on Monday. That you'll go back to Texas and I'll go back to New York, we'll have this great time that was ours. And I pray it will be enough, but I think, no I know I need more of you."

"Cordelia, what are you suggesting?"

She put her hands together and looked out at the ocean, "I'm suggesting that one week, every year we meet up. It doesn't have to be in the summer, it doesn't have to be in Coral Shore. It could be in Nebraska for all I care. But that one week, you and I are together. The rest of the year we live our separate lives. We go to the same place, at the same time each year. If one of us doesn't show up, then we know it's over, we've found someone new, we've moved on."

He couldn't believe she was suggesting it, "Cordelia, you can't be serious."

"I am. I've thought about it a lot. Now, I want you to think about it. You don't have to give me an answer yet. In fact, I don't want one until September 1st you can email me at the bakery. We don't have to mention this again. I've suggested it and now you get to think about it."

"Cordelia, do you really think you can do that? One week a year where we're together? What happens when you fall in love with someone else, you're not the kind of girl that cheats."

"Duke, I'm never going to love someone the way I love you." She confessed; the tears warm in her eyes as she fought to hold them in. "It's been eight years Duke and no other man has even gotten past a kiss goodnight. I'm not asking you to cheat on your eventual wife; I understand that when you get married our yearly date would be over. But wouldn't it be better than nothing?"

"It would be better than nothing." He hated that it was true, he was going to let her have her silly scheme, "Just not Nebraska, we need to go somewhere romantic, somewhere I can hide away in the world with you."

She laughed, "I didn't literally mean Nebraska, I wouldn't be caught dead there, I'm a CU girl after all."

Duke smiled, pulling her closer to him. She was happy, and he was going to do anything he could to keep her that way, even if it meant still not telling her that he was moving back to New York.

"We don't have to pick a place or time yet." She told him as they watched the ocean for a few minutes.

"We should get back to the house, clean up a bit before everyone shows up this afternoon." He suggested breathing in her scent.

"Just a few more minutes, please Duke, as soon as we get back to that house, we have to face everything, everyone."

"As you wish," He held onto her, enjoying the feel of her body against his, the warmth of the sun, the smell of the ocean.

♥

"We need to back off," James told Iris as they sat with Scottie on the deck.

"I know; I just fear that Cordelia is going to make a really stupid suggestion."

"Like what?"

Iris sighed as she looked up at him, "Meeting up with Duke once a year for a tryst."

"What happens if he tells her he's moving back to New York?"

"She freaks, I don't see her being thrilled about it." Iris confessed, "I don't know why, but I feel as though she'll be upset."

"Hello?" Beverly Watson's voice called out from the front of the house.

"Oh shit." Iris and James both said as they looked at each other.

"Cordelia, Iris, James, you guys here?" Tony called out, the voices getting closer to the deck.

"Out here!" James called out unable to stop himself.

"Hey, we came up early knowing Cordelia needed her airbrush stuff." Beverly carried the box of supplies, "Where is she?"

"She went for a walk on the beach." Iris choked on the words.

"Where's Duke?" Tony watched them; the way their eyes grew large.

"With her on the beach," Iris's voice was small.

"Good walk or bad walk?" Beverly studied them.

"No idea, I don't know what either of them is thinking." Iris breathed out, "Like one moment I think they're like doing really well, getting along and then the next something sets Cordelia off and she's mad and Duke goes to chase after her."

Tony nodded as he pulled out his phone, "So that's why I haven't seen a #CordukeReunion update since this?"

Iris and James looked at each other, "You know about that huh?"

"All of New York City knows." Beverly told them, "What were you two thinking?"

"It started as a goof between us and Gage, if you go all the way back to Monday night, you'll see that. We realized Cordelia didn't know about Duke being Gage's best man." James started.

"And we started tweeting about this epic reunion that was going to happen, with neither Cordelia nor Duke using Twitter we didn't think they would find out; I mean they haven't, yet."

"They will. People are talking about it." Beverly pulled up the article she'd read on her phone to show them.

"Oh no," James would recognize that mobile site in his sleep; it was the site he worked for. He scrolled up to see who was curating everything, "Crap. This took off more than we realized Iris."

"We figured they were going to be mad either way at us, so we might as well continue."

"Oh, you are, are you?" Tony pulled something up on his phone, "Look at these pictures, of course, people are interested."

"I love that one; they were so sweet dancing in the kitchen." Iris beamed.

"One thing I've been dying to know," Beverly put her arm around Iris as she led her to the kitchen, "Did they really break up because of a goat?"

"Oh yeah; only Cordelia, right?" Iris sighed, "That's probably what made this blow-up, how ridiculous that was. I don't know how she'll react to any of this."

Beverly shook her head, "I don't know either when it comes to Duke and their relationship, I've never known how she'll react to anything."

"She's convinced herself that Duke is going back to Texas and they'll never see each other again."

"You mean—never mind." Beverly stopped herself.

"That his clinic is going to be in your building, where he'll also be living?" Iris shook her head, "She doesn't want to think about what happens after Monday, she's convinced herself that she and Duke have this week together for a reason and after that, he's gone."

"She can believe in Pluto, but she can't believe in Duke?"

"She thinks she gave up the right to ask him to change his life when she sent the promise ring back, and of course she would never think to move to Texas, not like she would have to, but you know what I mean."

"Yeah, I love my daughter, but she's exhausting." Beverly sighed as she set the box of airbrushing supplies down on the counter.

♥

"Duke, it's good to see you." Tony pulled the younger man into a hug when he and Cordelia got up on the deck.

"Hi Mr. Watson, it's good to see you too."

"Dad, why are you here so early?"

"Mom wanted to make sure you got your supplies, so you had time to do your work." Tony hugged his daughter, "So, what were you two up to?"

"Just clearing the air, we're trying to be friends and put the past in the past," Cordelia explained.

Iris rolled her eyes and James elbowed her.

"I should go check and make sure I have everything I need if you'll excuse me." Cordelia made her way into the kitchen where she found her mother, "Hey Mom."

"Hey sweetie, I brought your stuff, are you sure you didn't need the modeling chocolate?"

"Yeah, Duke helped me make some." Cordelia gave her mother a hug, "How come you never told me he worked at the bakery?"

"You never asked; it didn't seem important." She told her daughter, "What do you still have to get done?"

Cordelia sighed, "Um I have to decorate the cake, the airbrushing, and Gage asked me to make some cookies for the dinner tonight. I just have to make sure I have everything."

"If you need help, I'm here."

"Thanks, Mom." Cordelia started towards the pantry.

"Cordelia are you sure you're okay. I know you and Duke haven't seen each other for a long time."

"Yeah, we cleared the air, I think. I thought he was dating a girl at school named Wanda, based on a picture one of his frat brothers posed on Facebook. Turns out, that Wanda was the goat and it was part of his Frat pledge."

"You mean like when the Gammas made you carry that cardboard Captain America around for a week calling him your boyfriend?"

"Something like that," she blushed, "We talked about it; I feel so stupid that I let him get away because I was so insecure. We're being friendly, we'll get along, we'll dance at the wedding if we have to."

"And in the kitchen perhaps?" Beverly asked, watching the way her daughter froze before slowly turning around, "Iris saw you, she told me."

"Iris has a lot of ideas running around in her head; she should focus some of that energy on her and James."

"What?"

"They have something gone on, but I don't know what exactly, and I don't think they know either."

"So, you're all still a bunch of confused kids huh?"

"Something like that." Cordelia sighed.

♥

"Okay Duke, real talk." Tony pulled him into the Library, "What's going on with you and Cordelia?"

"We're enjoying each other's company, Sir." Duke could feel the knot in his stomach move to his throat, "She isn't aware I'm moving back to New York, because when I've tried to tell her, she wouldn't let me. She just knows that on Monday I got back to Texas, and she thinks that's the last time she's ever going to see me."

Tony nodded, "And you think she'll be okay when she finds out you're in New York?"

"I think that Cordelia is going to be thrilled and maybe angry, but I believe in us Sir, I believe in Cordelia, the same way she believes in Pluto."

"So, what are your intentions with her Duke?" He watched the younger man, confidence in him different from what he'd always had.

"Well Sir, when I see Cordelia in New York I intend to propose to her. I would like your blessing for that. I love her Sir, I never stopped, and I know she loves me and never stopped."

"You know Duke; you came to me years ago, asking for my blessing to take her on her first date."

"Yes Sir, I did." He'd been so nervous that afternoon, and he'd been nervous on another afternoon. Right now, though, he wasn't nervous.

"And then a few years later you asked me for my blessing to ask her to marry you, I know you planned to do it on the first break from school."

"Yes, Sir; that I did."

"I gave you my blessing then, didn't I?"

"Yes, you sure did." Duke grew hopeful.

"So, I'm going to say you still have my blessing and I hope that it works out this time."

"So, do I, Sir, we've lost almost eight years together, I don't want to lose anymore."

"Good." Tony put a hand on Duke' shoulder and pointed to a manila envelope, "Also, Beverly told me to give you these, copies of your lease and your business paperwork, you got the name you wanted for the clinic, are you sure about that name?"

"Positive Sir." Duke took the packet of papers, "I will do everything I can to make her happy as long as she'll let me."

"I know you will Son." Tony hoped that everything worked out this time, he really did. He'd witness just how hollow Cordelia seemed without Duke in her life; he didn't want her to continue that way.

♥

Cordelia had finished making a list of things she needed and went upstairs to change so she could run to the store. Scottie was curled up on her unmade bed fast asleep. She couldn't believe that no one had claimed him yet. Maybe she would find a flyer about him being missing while she was out, though part of her hoped she didn't. She was already attached to the dog and ready to insist he get to stay in New York with her.

"Hi." Duke was in the doorway a smile on his face.

"Hi." She smiled at him, wondering how long he'd been there.

"Hey." He took the few steps towards her, cupping her face in his hands before kissing her. "I've been dying to do that since we got back from the beach."

Cordelia blushed, "What are you up to?"

"I'm going to clean up a bit, I have to go over some paperwork about my clinic, but it shouldn't take too long. What about you?"

"I'm going to run to the market and pick up a few things I need for the cookies Gage asked me to make. I also need more powdered sugar for the cake."

"So, you want some company?" His voice was hopeful.

She bit her lower lip, "Normally I would say yes, but my Mom is coming with me."

"Well I'll be here, and if you need a bakery assistant, please come find me."

She kissed his cheek, "I will."

He watched her leave before he went into his room. He pulled out the papers that Beverly had drawn up for him, everything seemed to be what they had talked about already, and he got the name he wanted for his clinic. He stuffed them back in the envelope and put them at the bottom of his suitcase.

He grabbed his laptop and started to go through his emails, he had far more than he was expecting, including a bunch from people had hadn't talked to in years; Frat Brothers, college friends, people from high school. Why had everyone suddenly decided to email him?

That was when he saw the subject lines, "A GOAT?" "#CORDUKEREUNION"

He stared at them for a moment before he started to go through them, trying to figure out what was going on.

TO: DUKE SHAW
FROM: CLAUDIA ADAMS
SUBJECT: Oops, Sorry!
Duke, I am so sorry that your girlfriend back then thought something was going on between us, and that she thought I was Wanda. Good Luck winning her back; it's obvious that the two of you are really in love.
#CordukeReunion
Claudia

TO: DUKE
FROM: OSCAR
SUBJECT: #CordukeReunion
Longtime Duke, way to go in getting the girl of your dreams. I can't wait to see this live before my eyes on Gage's big day.
Oscar

"What the hell is #CordukeReunion?"

TO: DUKE SHAW
FROM: NOAH WILSON
SUBJECT: Cordelia Watson
You know, part of me wasn't sure what to think when you got on Cordelia's phone the other night. I guess the Cowboy finally

decided he wants the Princess. If I hadn't seen the pictures or the videos, I wouldn't believe it.

Don't worry; I'll pick up the pieces when you break her heart again.

Noah

"Videos, pictures, what am I missing?"

TO: DUKE SHAW ZGN Lil' Bro
FROM: CARTER PENGRASS ZGN Big Bro
SUBJECT: Wanda

Dude, that's why you got dumped your freshmen year because I tagged Wanda as your girlfriend in a picture? I am so sorry about that man, but you've got to admit it's hilarious, the guys at our old house think it's a riot.

C.P.

TO: Duke
FROM: Paige
SUBJECT: Cordelia and Duke forever!

I can't believe how happy you and Cordelia look together in those pictures that Iris and James have been posting on Twitter. The two of you are a viral sensation; everyone is rooting for you (okay, probably not Noah Wilson, but he's creepy). Good luck Shaw, you and Cordelia deserve to be happy.

NYCBuzz.com/7/1378/cordukereunion/

He clicked the link, discovering a catalog of tweets that had started Monday night from Iris, James, even Gage.

He read them all, it was everything that had happened so far, they had pictures of him and Cordelia together, including one from that morning asleep on the deck.

What the hell had his friends been thinking?

They couldn't have thought this was a good idea, could they?

He closed his laptop, not wanting to imagine what else the people who were supposed to be his and Cordelia's best friends would share with the rest of the world next.

Scottie came up to him and Duke grabbed the leash, he would walk the dog until he didn't want to punch someone.

"Hey, Duke where you are going?" James called out as he sat on the kitchen island eating an apple while Tony and Iris were discussing something at the table.

Duke stopped and Scottie stayed close to him, "#CordukeReunion?"

"Uh oh," James looked to Iris, both frozen, not sure what Duke was going to do.

"I want to believe that the three of you meant well when you started it, but right now my email is full of messages from people about this, including Noah Wilson"

"Cheese Soufflé!" Iris said, "Sorry, reflex."

"Guys, my relationship with Cordelia is just that, mine. You need to stop with the tweeting or whatever it is your doing." Duke looked down at Scottie, "This weekend isn't about me and Cordelia, it's about Gage and Lauren. Any stolen moments Cordelia and I may or may not have are between us, now Scottie and I are going for a walk until I don't want to put my fist through the drywall."

Iris, James and Tony watched as Duke descended the deck stairs, "So, how are you going to fix this?"

Iris and James looked to each other, "What do you suggest?"

"Honesty, I feel that this place is thick with it, it's just hiding in the words people don't want to say."

"You're still teaching us, aren't you Watson?" Iris whined.

"Always."

♥

Cordelia sat in the kitchen while she finished decorating the cake with the icing and chocolate flowers. She was at peace, meditative even as she worked, she smiled to herself. She had something to look forward to, the next few days when she could steal time away with Duke, celebrating one of her best friends getting married, and then if she allowed herself to believe it was possible, she would have a whole week with Duke in the future, and it could be something she could look forward to every year.

The deck door slid open and she could hear Scottie's paws on the floor. She looked up, shocked to see that Duke appeared upset. She finished what she was doing before putting the piping bag down, "Hey, are you okay?"

"Where is everybody?"

"No idea, they were all gone when Mom and I got back. She's upstairs to take a nap since they got up so early." She wiped her hands on a towel, "Duke, what's wrong?"

"Can you take a break; we need to talk."

Cordelia felt a knot twist in her stomach, "Yeah, let me put this back in the walk in."

"I'll meet you in your room, come on Scottie."

"Of course," Cordelia watched him disappear up the back steps before wheeling the cake into the walk in. Suddenly she was losing the hope that had just filled her only moments before.

As she climbed the steps slowly, she was thankful that she'd finished the cake except for the airbrushing. Her hands were shaking as she opened the door of her room; Duke was sitting on the bed, Scottie's head resting in his lap.

"I checked my email today while you were out."

Cordelia nodded, not sure she understood what that had to do with her, "Okay, so?"

"I'm betting if you were to check yours, you would have lots of the same types of emails, I'm sure Oscar, Paige, and Noah didn't just email me."

"Why would any of them email either of us?" She sat next to him, trying to understand what he was trying to tell her.

"Because you and I are a viral sensation on Twitter and NYCBuzz.com"

"What, how is that possible?"

Duke took a deep breath, trying to stay calm, "Iris, James, and even Gage started tweeting about us on Monday night. They used the hashtag, Corduke Reunion."

"I don't understand, what were they saying?"

"Apparently, they were excited to find out what happened when we were face to face." He reached for her hand, thankful she let him pick it up, he already felt calmer with her around. He kissed her temple, "Let me get my laptop, I'll show you some of what I saw."

Cordelia tried to process what had happened; her friends had taken her and Duke's story and shared it with the world.

"Start here; it's the day before we saw each other."

Cordelia looked at the screen, so many tweets screen capped. Who would take the time to do this? She looked up at Duke, "I don't understand what they were doing."

Duke ran his hand over his hair before laying back on her bed, "I think maybe this started out just between them, I don't know, it looks like they're just going back and forth with each other really."

"Tweeted by James Sheath; Today is the day! They'll reunite on the train, bet she falls into his arms @IrisLaArt #CordukeReunion" Cordelia read out loud, "And then a picture from James of me falling into your arms a few tweets later after they made another bet."

She started to scroll down the page, "Oh my God, they posted a picture of Wanda."

"Yup, and us dancing, oh and my favorite is at the end."

Cordelia was afraid as she scrolled further down, "That's us, asleep on the deck this morning. You have to go before my father kills you."

"He won't."

"Duke, you know how he is." Her eyes filled with pure concern.

"I do, and I'm not worried about that. I'm worried about you, now that our personal, private relationship has been tweeted to the whole world." He took the laptop, putting it on the bed behind them.

Cordelia was silent for a moment, "I think that it got away from them, they meant no harm. They love us Duke and we love them. It also shows me that we need to keep our moments, between us. Though I'm sure they might still catch something. It doesn't matter. You're going back to Texas and I'm going back to New York. What we have is this, here and now. Which includes the cookies I still must bake, and don't you and James have to get some ribs going?"

Duke sighed, "You sure you're okay?"

"Yeah, did Noah really email you?"

"Yeah, he did see?" Duke pulled the computer back from behind them, letting Cordelia read it.

Cordelia started to type him a reply.

"What are you doing?"

"Something I should've done a long time again.

TO: NOAH WILSON
FROM: DUKE SHAW
SUBJECT: RE: Cordelia Watson

155

Noah,
Duke never broke my heart. I broke his.
Aren't you tired of being used by me as I pretend, I'm moving on?
New York is filled with a lot of women, a lot of women that would appreciate you. Don't you think you deserve that?
You won't have any pieces to pick up; because Duke told you the other night we're back together. He has always had my heart and I've always had his.
I think it's time you move on, and time to find a new bakery; I could list several that are much closer to your office.
Goodbye,
Cordelia

Duke read it from over her shoulder, "So I've always had your heart?"

"You always have, you always will."

He kissed her, "If I didn't have to go start those ribs . . ."

"And if I didn't have to bake those cookies . . ."

"And your father wasn't just down the hall, sure to burst into this room any moment . . ."

"Tonight, you and me, we forget the rest of the world."

"Perfect, let's get our stuff done."

♥

Duke prepared the grill on the deck, still no sign of Iris, James or Tony anywhere. Beverly had come down to look for him, admitting she knew about the NYCBuzz article and of course the tweets, encouraging them to put an end to it.

She was now down at the beach, on the phone with her son making sure that everything was okay at the house and bakery.

"Duke," Beverly called over to him, "I just talked to Scott, the painters finished your apartment this morning, and they'll have the clinic done by Monday."

"Thank you so much."

"No problem, they said your artwork arrived for the windows."

"Great." Duke looked towards the kitchen, "When is it going up?"

"Tuesday morning, the day you leave Texas." Beverly looked towards her daughter, "Before Tony and I got married, I was scared, I didn't always believe in us, but Tony did. A lot of the time she takes after him, sometimes even her Uncle Casper, but she does take after me, and I see it now. I understand why you haven't told her, I might not like it, but I do get it."

Duke checked the settings on the grill before he looked to Beverly, "I fear that saying goodbye for a week to pack up would somehow make it harder for her then letting her think it's forever."

"I heard you asked for Tony's blessing again are you sure?"

"Mrs. Watson, Beverly, I'm surer about that than anything else in the world."

She looked to make sure that Cordelia was occupied, "Well, this arrived last night from your Grandpa, I don't expect you to use it yet, in fact, wait, make James take Iris to dinner in Williamsburg, it would be a good date for the two of them, they should have an actual date."

"You know about that?" Duke felt her place the small black box in his hand and immediately he knew what it was. His grandfather had held onto it for all this time, "Did you look at it."

"Yes, I know, it's obvious. They might need a little push towards the more traditional aspect of the relationship. And yes, the ring is gorgeous; you really had him hold onto that for you?"

"Yeah, I always knew once I finished school I was going to come back to New York and do whatever I could to win her back." He watched as Cordelia scooped cookie dough onto trays, "Do you ever just watch her while she's baking? The way she glows, it's amazing."

Beverly watched her daughter for a moment before watching the way Duke watch her, "Good luck."

"Thank you." Duke slipped the box into his pocket before he went back to attending to the grill.

♥

After Cordelia put the cookies in the oven she looked out to the deck, watching as Duke manned the grill.

"Cordelia, Duke, Iris, James, you guys here?" Gage called out, finally, he arrived.

"In the kitchen Gage!" Cordelia called in response as she started cleaning up.

"I'm so glad you're here." He told her before wrapping her into a tight hug.

"I know about the tweets Gage, so does Duke."

He backed up, "It was mostly James and Iris."

"I'm not exactly mad; I don't think you guys meant any harm by it." She let her glare soften.

"Where's everyone else?" He relaxed for a moment.

"Duke is making sure you get real Texas ribs, my Mom was somewhere, and the others disappeared after Duke confronted them about the tweets." Cordelia looked around, "Where are your parents, Lauren, her family?"

"They'll get here later; they had a few more things to do in the city before they could get out here." Gage couldn't help but notice the smile on his best friends face, he'd seen her in so much pain in middle school over Duke, and then the last eight years, he was glad they were finally figuring things out, "So since I've only gotten to know what's up from the tweets, why don't you tell me what's up?"

"That's between Cordelia and Me." Duke was at the deck door, his arms crossed over his chest as he looked at his best friend.

"Duke!" Gage hugged him, "I'm sorry about the tweets, I don't think any of us meant for it to go viral like that."

"I'm sure you didn't, but Cordelia and I are going to keep anything that might be happening between us."

Gage nodded, "You know you have to dance together at the wedding, right?"

"We're aware, I'm sure Iris or James will snap a picture and it will get added to the others." Cordelia wore oven mitts on her hands as she waited in front of the oven.

"So, something is going on."

"Gage!" They both replied.

"Sorry, I just love both of you, and I want you to be happy. And I think you guys have a chance now—."

"Gage, come join me on the deck, let's leave Cordelia to her baking." Duke grabbed his friend, dragging him outside, "She doesn't know I'm moving back."

"She doesn't, I thought Iris and James were kidding about that."

"She won't let me tell her. She keeps telling me I'm going back to Texas and that Monday she and I are over."

"That's ridiculous."

"You know that I know that, everyone else knows that, but it's what Cordelia needs to believe right now."

"Won't she be mad when she realizes you kept this from her?"

"Maybe, but I'm hoping that she is more thrilled to see me," Duke confessed.

Gage looked around, "Where's the dog?"

"Up in Cordelia's room, Scottie is well behaved, but no one's reported him to the animal shelters as missing or put up any fliers that any of us have seen."

"Well I guess Cordelia's getting a dog since you know, you're going back to Texas." Gage teased.

"Yeah, I was kind of thinking that." A smile crossed Duke' lips.

"You have a plan, don't you?"

"Well, I was just thinking that since I'll be in Texas and Scottie will be in New York with Cordelia, he will really need to be chipped, and there will be an Animal Clinic in the same building."

"Cordelia brings him in, and there you are."

"Yeah, she'll be mad, but she'll be happy."

Gage watched the way his friend's eyes danced when he spoke of the woman he loved, "I hope I get to see it."

"Why, are you going to Instagram Live the whole thing?"

"That would be brilliant." Gage teased, "But I won't, your moment with Cordelia should be your moment."

"At least I don't have to worry about you stealing it this time."

"That's right, you don't." Gage looked inside, "Does she know you love her?"

"She won't let me actually say it, but she knows. If I say it, I think it makes it harder for her to say goodbye, and she needs to be able to do that."

"Good things come to those who wait." Gage looked out to the beach, "Oh look, Iris, James, and T-Bone!"

"It's safe to come up here, I've calmed down. Cordelia isn't mad either." Duke called out as he opened the grill to check that everything was going okay so far.

"Well glad to hear that man, we're sorry. It was really just the three of us joking around." James explained.

"Now last time I checked this weekend is about this guy and his future wife, so shouldn't we focus on him? James is everything set in the basement for our Video Game marathon tonight?" Duke patted Gage on the back as he looked at the others.

"Off to go work on that now." James waved as he left to go inside.

"I should probably go talk to Cordelia." Iris snapped her fingers as she walked into the house.

"T-Bone! I'm so glad you're here."

"Gage, do you really think I would miss this? I've known you since preschool, back when you wanted to marry Cordelia and Iris. I'm happy that you found Lauren, you've been good for each other."

"Secret of life." Gage smiled.

"Exactly," Tony looked around, "Is Cordelia really okay?"

"I think so Sir, she knows they didn't mean any harm. She did send Noah an interesting email from my account, told him he wouldn't be picking up the pieces of her heart since it belongs to me." Duke couldn't help but smile.

"Part of me wants to chase you off this deck, but part of me is thrilled to hear that. Be good to her."

"I will Sir."

♥

Cordelia was filling her airbrush with food coloring when she saw Iris come in, walking towards her, "Hey, I saw some very interesting tweets today."

"I heard Duke was pissed, glad he calmed down." Iris sat on the stool, watching her friend as she tested her equipment, "I know your relationship with him is yours, and we're supposed to butt out or whatever, bur Cordelia he loves you. He's loved you for years."

Cordelia didn't say anything.

"What would be the perfect situation for you and Duke?"

Cordelia looked up, "What do you mean?"

"I mean, would it be him moving to New York, you moving to Texas, or once a year a week of pretending you're not missing him like crazy?"

"In a perfect world I would love for him and me to be together, him in New York, or me in Texas, but we don't live in a perfect world. I can't give up my business, and I can't ask him to give up his. We have what we have, and that's the last I'm going to say about it."

"Okay, I was just curious." Iris sighed, wondering how much longer she could keep this secret.

"I need to get this done," Cordelia told her friend as she started to focus on the airbrush again, painting the roses first yellow, then pink as everything blended together.

"I'm going to go set up for our Pre-Wedding movie party tonight." Iris excused herself, hoping to God that Cordelia would stop being so stubborn.

♥

When Cordelia finished the cake, she pushed the cart back into the walk-in before starting to clean up her supplies. Duke came in from outside, "Hey, I was watching you work; I think that's becoming one of my favorite things."

"Oh please, I really don't think to watch me paint a cake is that entertaining."

"You would be surprised." He quickly kissed her cheek, "What are you up to now?"

"Well, besides cleaning up my supplies, I thought I might go help Iris set up for our movie night. What did you have in mind?"

"Shucking corn, helping make dinner, James has abandoned me."

Cordelia smiled, "I think I can help with that."

Duke was already gathering the things they needed when they heard more voices, "I think everyone else arrived."

Lauren Ricci entered the kitchen, her long dark hair pulled back into a bun, she wore slim wire-framed glasses, "Cordelia, is it done?"

"Come with me." Cordelia grabbed her friends' hand and led her to the walk in, opening the door, letting her see the cake.

Lauren didn't speak for a moment as she looked at the cake, "It's exactly what we wanted. Thank you, Cordelia."

"You're welcome." Cordelia gave her a quick hug, "I think Gage is around somewhere, Duke I are getting dinner ready."

"Great, I'll see you in a little bit, Third Wheel, nice to see you again."

Duke grew red, "Every time she sees me, she still calls me that."

"Aww, it's sweet, she's kidding though."

"I know." Duke was preparing a pot of water for the corn, "So, she liked the cake?"

"It was exactly what she wanted." Cordelia smiled as she started shucking the corn.

Duke turned the radio on, but not a single slow song played while they worked. Instead, they were greeted with 90s pop.

"Cor, we are all set for later tonight except the popcorn which we'll make then. Oh, hey, Duke, what's up?"

"Where's your boyfriend, he should be helping me make dinner instead of Cordelia."

Iris froze, "Who?"

"Oh, wow Duke, I'm not sure I've ever seen this look from Iris before." She circled around her friend, "Iris, hello."

"I don't have a boyfriend."

"Then what is James?"

"He's James, now I think I'm going to take your dog for a walk and get out of here." She paused, "Are my Mom and Dennis here yet?"

"No idea, I just saw Lauren." Cordelia shrugged.

"Thank you, Scottie would like it very much if he got to go for a walk with his Auntie Iris." Duke shot Cordelia a look who came over to him, her arms around him.

"Can you believe it; I think you actually stunned her." She spoke a moment later.

"I haven't seen a reaction like that since actually, never."

Before they could say anything, else Iris had Scottie on the leash following her to the door; and James wasn't far behind. He stopped to look at his friends, "What did you say to her?"

"Duke just asked where her boyfriend was, where were you, James?" Cordelia tilted her head with a smile as she looked at him.

"We're not boyfriend and girlfriend, we are James and Iris, and whatever that is is between us—oh, you're still good. I get it now. I'll go catch up with her. Good one Duke, good one."

"I think we're going to be good the rest of the week after that." Duke started to rinse the vegetables for the salad, "Are you okay, you didn't get much sleep this morning."

"I'm fine, it'll actually be kind of good this way, I'll go to bed at a sort of normal-ish hour, maybe." She couldn't keep the smile off her face, "Well we do have a busy day tomorrow, the rehearsal in the afternoon, the cocktail party with the rest of the guests, and then the day after that is the wedding."

"We're in the home stretch." Cordelia trailed off, thinking about how soon this would all end, "but I can't wait to see the look on Gage's face when he sees Lauren in her dress. Just an FYI you might have to catch him."

"I'm prepared to do so."

"Where do you maybe want to meet when we're done with our activities?" She looked up from the bread she was slicing.

"Our bathroom, trust me." He kissed her forehead before leaving to check on the ribs.

♥

"Iris!" James called out as he ran after her and Scottie on the beach before finally catching up to them, "They were just teasing us, showing us how it felt."

"I know." She sighed as she sat down in the sand, Scottie jumping around her, "I just feel guilty."

James sat next to her, "Because we haven't told them, or because we—?"

"We haven't told them, or anyone." She looked up at the sky, "I mean besides your family."

"We should talk to your Mom and Dennis when they get in." James took her hand, "They should know first, and then we can tell Cordelia, Gage, and Duke."

Iris smiled, "I love you."

He pushed her blonde hair away from her eyes, "I love you too. How scared of Dennis should I be?"

"I don't think you have to worry about that." She rested her head on his shoulder, "I'd be more worried about Cordelia's reaction."

"Butterscotch won't hurt me, she'll threaten me, but she won't hurt me. Will she?"

Iris laughed, "I think you'll be okay."

"Good." He pulled her closer. "We're never going to hear the end of this, are we? They're exhausting."

CHAPTER 7

Dennis Wagner looked over to his wife Samantha, and then back at his stepdaughter and the young man with her. He didn't know what to say, so he looked back to Samantha.

Samantha Lange-Wagner was speechless for a long moment before the words finally came to her, "I'm not exactly surprised by this. I think on some level I knew this would happen. If the two of you are happy, I think we can support this."

"Yes, of course." Dennis agreed, his mind still reeling from the secret he'd just been told, "We do wish you could've let us in on this sooner."

"Mr. Wagner just know that I love Iris more than I ever thought I could. I never expected to find a love like this, and with my best friend." James held Iris's hand tightly.

"I know you're shocked Mom, Dennis, but every time we tried to even bring this up, something stopped us. But we realize now we were being a bit selfish in keeping this between us."

Samantha and Dennis were both still in shock, processing, "I love you both, you are good for each other. We've said that for years, haven't we Dennis."

"Yes, yes we have." He blinked several times before saying the only thing he could think of, "Be good to each other."

Iris and James both smiled, "Um, could we just keep this between us for a little while longer?"

Samantha and Dennis took each other's hand and nodded, "Of course baby girl."

"Great, we'll see you at dinner." Iris and James rose from the couch and left the Library.

Dennis and Samantha continued to sit in silence looking at each other and then away every so often, finally, he spoke, "Are we sure this is real and they're not just joking with us?"

Samantha sighed, "I think they're serious. I mean I suspected something was going on with them since college, but I was not expecting this."

Dennis hugged his wife, "It'll be okay, they'll tell their friends and then we can publicly freak out."

"James's a nice boy, right?" Samantha questioned, even though she already knew the answer.

"Yeah," Dennis thought back on all the interactions with him over the years, and that

Tony always said James was a good kid. "I mean, he would have to be right. Look at that group of friends, if he wasn't, he wouldn't be a part of it."

"I just wish they had told us sooner."

Dennis kissed her forehead, "I know, but we can't change the past, we can only hope to have a good future."

♥

Dinner was filled with laughter and old stories, going back as far as when the parents were kids growing up together. When the meal was over the men found their way down to the basement where they planned to play the latest video games until their eyes hurt, while the women went upstairs to watch the movies Iris and Cordelia had picked up the day before.

"Which one do you want to watch first?" Iris held up the selection.

"Let's go with When Harry Met Sally," Lauren made her pick and it wasn't long before they were all engrossed in watching Billy Crystal and Meg Ryan dance around their feelings for each other.

As the movie got close to the end Cordelia leaned over to Iris, "I hope that James realizes what he could have with you."

"Shh, movie" Iris replied, not wanting to discuss it just yet.

Cordelia found herself lost in the ending as Harry ran through the streets of New York City, on New Year's Eve to find Sally, declare his love for her, "They don't make guys like Harry anymore, do they?"

"Oh sweetie," Beverly looked to her daughter, "Harry was afraid of his feelings for Sally."

"Because she pushed him away for so long, that by the time they slept together she didn't realize she was in love with him, and by then the friendship was ruined." Iris sat up and started to pick her nail polish. "Can you really be friends with someone and then become more?"

"It happens; you just have to be open to it." Jennifer Keller told her from the chaise seat of the sectional couch that was the central seating area of the media room.

"Be open to it Iris," Lauren told her, "You never know what you're missing out on."

"Is it time for the next movie?" Iris asked as the credits were rolling.

"Yes, let's go with this one." Beverly set up The Princess Bride, before finding her seat on the couch again.

Cordelia hugged a pillow as she watched, "That day she was amazed to discover that when he was saying 'As you wish', what he meant was 'I love you.'"

Cordelia let the pillow go, this was one of Duke' favorite movies, she remembered that now. He kept saying 'As you wish' to her. Was he trying to tell her something he didn't think she could handle or wanted to hear?

For the rest of the movie she chewed on red gummi bears while her mind raced, far too many conversations included that phrase the last few days.

When the movie ended the mothers all excused themselves, leaving the three girls alone.

"Cor, are you okay?" Iris wasn't sure what had kept her so still during the movie besides each handful of gummi bears she grabbed.

"Duke loves me." Cordelia finally breathed.

Lauren looked to Iris, "Of course he loves you; didn't you know that already?"

"He's not saying it straight out; he's using the line from the movie." Cordelia picked up a handful of M&Ms from the bowl and another handful of popcorn, tossing both into her mouth as she paced around the media room.

"So, is that a bad thing?"

"Yes, no, I don't know." Cordelia sat down, "I'm confused."

"Just let this weekend be what it is." Lauren told her, "Make no promises, and let fate guide you."

"Thanks, Lauren, that's great advice."

"If you and Duke are meant to have a future together, fate will provide it."

"This isn't your normal genius type answer." Iris took a sip of her soda.

Lauren shrugged, "I've learned that science and logic don't always provide the answers for our heart. Sometimes we have to believe that it's a greater force."

"Aww Lauren, we really did teach you something." Cordelia beamed for a moment.

"That you did, Maid of Honor." Lauren gave Cordelia a quick hug, "Don't over think it. You tend to do that."

"Thanks, so now that the mothers are gone who says we check out Magic Mike XXL?" Iris waved the movie in front of them.

"Let's do it."

♥

Duke realized it had been a while since he'd played a video game, he wasn't even sure he could remember the last time he turned his gaming system on. He'd been so busy with school, work, everything he never had time. After a few hours, he ducked out, took Scottie for a walk and then decided to just wait for Cordelia to be done with movie night.

The alone time gave him a little chance to start putting together the documents he needed for the clinic and try to go through his emails and he soon realized his texts and even Facebook messages. It seemed everyone he knew had read the NYCBuzz article.

He got sick of staring at a screen and put it all away when he went into the bathroom and started to fill the tub with water and bubbles. He grabbed some of the flameless candles he'd used the night before and set them up around the bathroom, clearing the room of any dirty towels or clothes that might have been left behind.

He was starting to worry that the water would get cold when he heard Cordelia's door open.

"Duke?" She called out as she walked through her room, a smile plastered on her face.

He met her at the doorway, "You look happy, I thought you ladies were watching sappy movies."

"And Magic Mike XXL." Cordelia beamed.

"Oh, so you prefer what Channing Tatum?"

Cordelia reached out, her fingers resting on his hard t-shirt clad chest, "I mean Magic Mike, that's a fantasy. You're real, right in front of me. How could I want that, when I have you?"

Duke smiled, "Good answer, now close your eyes and trust me."

"Okay." Cordelia did as she was told, feeling Duke guide her into the bathroom.

He stood behind her and waited for just a moment, "Open your eyes."

Cordelia slowly did and couldn't believe what she saw, candles and a bubble bath, "Duke, you didn't have to do this."

"I know, but I thought you could use one." He kissed the back of her neck, "I know it's been a stressful few days, and I wanted to do something special for you."

"You are going to spoil me, Duke Shaw, how is a girl supposed to survive without you preparing bubble baths, or sprinkling rose petals on the bed?"

Duke spun her around to look at him, "You are to hold onto these moments Cordelia, know that you deserve them. That any man who wouldn't do these kinds of things for you isn't worthy of you." He kissed her before she could argue.

"You know," Cordelia looked up into his peridot eyes, knowing she could lose herself in them forever, "The tub is big enough for two."

"You think so huh?"

She nodded, "Why don't you join me in the tub and afterward we could do something really crazy."

"What would that be?"

"We put on our pajamas, and crawl into bed together, and just hold each other for a while. That's what I need and want from you, Duke."

"As you wish" He could see the flicker of knowledge in her barn wood eyes as he spoke.

Cordelia pulled away and started to undress, her eyes on Duke as he did so as well, "See you have something that Magic Mike doesn't."

"What's that?"

"You're real and you're here." She took his hand, "And you have that great little dime sized tattoo."

They climbed into the tub slowly, the water still hot as they settled in, Cordelia relaxing her body against Duke. His fingers trailed up her arms to her shoulders where he began to massage them, enjoy the soft moans of pleasure she released without thinking.

He kissed her neck, nibbled her earlobe, his hands traveling down her body.

Cordelia turned around slowly so not to splash water out of the tub before capturing his mouth with hers, her fingers teasing his hard chest before she let her hand slip under the water, her fingers wrapping around his hard cock.

"Cordelia," He breathed, "What are you doing?"

"Shh," She kissed his neck, "Just relax."

"Wasn't that what I was trying to get you to do?"

"Trust me."

"As you wish"

Cordelia kissed him as her hand pumped him under the bubbles, she could feel his body react, the way his breath caught, his abs tenses and she felt him release into the tub.

"That was something." He finally said as he watched her wipe her hand off with a hand towel, "I wasn't expecting that."

"Well, you're not the only one full of surprises. Let's get out, it's getting cold."

"Good idea."

They wrapped themselves in the large fluffy towels and before Cordelia knew what was happening, Duke picked her up and carried her into his bedroom.

"Duke Shaw, what are you doing?"

"Taking you to bed Cordelia Watson," He gently laid her down and undid her towel, his mouth on hers before she could bring up pajamas.

"Did I awake a beast in you?" She asked as he took her nipple in his mouth to suckle.

"Tell me to stop and I will." He told her as he looked into her soulful eyes.

"Make love to me Duke, don't hold back." She reached for his towel, letting it drop on the foot of the bed and before either one knew it, they were deep in the ecstatic pleasure that was each other.

"Pajama's now?" He asked as he continued to kiss her neck.

"Yes, I'm going to get something from the kitchen, I'll be back in a few minutes. You better be in your pajamas by then Duke." She warned as she wrapped the towel around her body before going into her room and quickly pulling on her shorts and tank top.

In the kitchen, she found the bottle of wine they had started the day before and a bowl of strawberries.

"That looks romantic."

Cordelia turned to see Gage sitting on the kitchen counter eating one of the cookies she'd made him earlier. "Just a little late-night snack."

"How many glasses Cordelia?" He opened the cabinet, "One or two?"

"Two, Gage, don't make a big deal about this, please."

"I won't." He handed her the two glasses, "I think the two of you belong together, I always have. I hope you figure out a way to make it happen."

"Thank you; wait why are you still up?"

"Video games, we're still playing. James and your Dad right now are killing it."

"Really?"

"Yeah, I needed a break, Duke gave up hours ago, I think he missed you. Or he just wants to spend as much time with you as possible; you know eight years and all since the goat came between you."

Cordelia threw a strawberry at him, "That is going to haunt me forever, isn't it?"

"Yes, but only because we love you," Gage picked up another cookie and headed towards the basement, "Have fun, Cordelia."

When she got back to the bedroom Duke was in blue plaid pajama bottoms and a pale blue t-shirt. Why did he always look so damn good in blue?

"Something wrong?" He asked as he got up to help her with what she was carrying.

"No, everything right now is about as close to perfect as it could be."

Duke poured the wine into the glasses and watched as Cordelia took the bowl of strawberries to the middle of the bed, logically he knew not every night would be filled with the romance of candles, rose petals or bubble baths, but he hoped to God their future would have these little moments like this.

"What are you thinking about?" She accepted a glass and looked up at him.

"Just thinking of how perfect this moment is, how lucky I am."

Cordelia blushed, "I think I'm the lucky one, I am after all the one who dumped you over a goat, you forgave me for that."

"Yeah, they're not going to let you live that down."

"I don't think anyone will thank us for being a viral sensation. Remind me to send James and Iris an edible arrangement."

Duke smiled, "Well, just think about all the private moments between us that the rest of the world will never know about, like our bubble that."

"That would really kill your street cred, wouldn't it, Mad Dog."

"It sure would Princess Dancing Sunshine."

"Aww, you remembered."

"Of courses."

"Mardi Gras, senior year. . ." She bit into a strawberry as she looked to him.

"Yeah, we were actually supposed to meet up with a group of Gamma Girls from Colorado."

"You were our Texas Zeta's we couldn't find." She smiled.

"You know, I was thinking about that one week a year thing you suggested."

Cordelia held her wine glass to her lips for a moment before taking a sip, "You were?"

"I was, now you mentioned going to the same place each year, but what's the fun in that? I want to explore new places with you, Cordelia. What if we pick a place each year, one year we could check out South Dakota, see Mount Rushmore and Crazy Horse, and then another year we go someplace like Memphis, or anywhere."

"That's a wonderful idea." She smiled, he took her seriously, it wouldn't be perfect, but maybe they did have some sort of future.

He brushed her hair away from her eyes, "What time do you need to be awake?"

"Five, I promised Mrs. Keller that I would have freshly baked muffins and some quick bread for breakfast."

"Well then, we should get to sleep. We've got baking to do in the morning."

Cordelia placed her empty wine glass on the nearest nightstand before finding herself wrapped in Duke' arms. "You know it's going to be difficult to not have you assist me."

"It's going to be weird not baking with you." He kissed the side of her head.

"I don't want to think about that now." She wrapped her arms around his, "Tell me a story Duke, one with a happy ending."

"Once Upon a time, there was this beautiful princess named Cordelia. She lived in a magical city, she had a best friend that was fiercely loyal, and overprotective father, a mother who knew when to let her spread her wings, and a younger brother who was just as protective, if not more so as her father. She was a little klutzy, but it was adorable. One day she fell into the lap of a cowboy, who had never seen someone smile as honestly as she did.

"The cowboy was lost and confused, but the princess helped him find his way, and the secret of life, people change people. One day they realized they were in love with each other, and after a few complications they were together . . . until a goat came between them." He looked down to see she was fast asleep, good he didn't want to spoil the ending for her. ♥

When the alarm on Duke's phone went of Cordelia's eyes flew open and it took her a moment to realize she was in Duke' embrace and had slept what might be the most normal hours she'd slept in years. It would be easy to do if she had Duke with her each night.

"Morning Cordelia" He'd already turned off the alarm as he was sitting up, "We've got a busy day ahead of us."

"That we do, so many more people are going to arrive." She sighed as she stretched her body, knowing that they would have far fewer chances to have stolen moments together.

Scottie came running into the room once he realized that his two favorite people were awake. "Okay, you and me Scottie, we'll let Cordelia do her thing while we go for a quick beach walk." Duke slipped on his sneakers and grabbed the leash.

"I'll meet you in the kitchen." She kissed his cheek, promising herself that today was going to be an amazing day, and tomorrow would be even better.

After she'd gotten ready, she made her way to the kitchen where she started gathering the ingredients needed, preheating the oven, and prepping the pans.

When Duke found his way down after putting Scottie back in the bedroom, he helped her and when everything was in the oven, he turned the radio on, the volume just loud enough that only the two of them could hear.

They swayed together, enjoying the serenity of the house that in a few hours would be filled with people. Right now, the only two were Cordelia and Duke.

"Are you going to save any dances for me at the wedding, or is your dance card full?"

"I think I might have a slot or two available for you." She rested her head on his shoulder as they continued to dance.

When the timer went off for the muffins Cordelia sighed as she pulled away from Duke, knowing that it wouldn't be long before everyone else was awake, ready to start the big rehearsal day.

♥

"Okay, the hard part is done." Iris sat in the middle of the bed watching as James dressed for the day.

"No, telling your parents was easy. How the hell are we going to tell our friends about this?"

"No idea." She confessed, "I mean this isn't something you just blurt out. To be honest, I kind of thought Dennis would've told Tony, who would've said something to Beverly, and it would just be out already."

James finished dressing and lay on the bed next to her, "Tonight, after dinner, we're having a bonfire on the beach. Let's just tell them then. The worst thing possible they get mad and toss us into the ocean."

Iris smiled, "They're going to be so mad at us."

"I think the secret is what's going to make them mad, why did we keep this a secret anyway?"

"I don't know it's always just been between us." She kissed him, "Just remember I love you."

"I'll never forget that." He kissed her again.

♥

The morning flew by with errands before the rehearsal and the dinner. After dinner, Lauren was exhausted and excused herself to try and get to sleep early. All the parents had gone somewhere to talk about the good old days, or at least that's what Dennis said they would be doing as he led Samantha out of the room behind Tony and Beverly.

The five friends had gone down to the beach, James and Duke building a bonfire as the sun started to set, and the darkness of night closed over them.

"Well fake ex-husband, are you nervous?" Cordelia smiled as she sat next to Duke, feeling his arms around her, just like in the past.

Gage stood up, looking at his friend, "No, I have you guys here with me, and I know that I want to spend the rest of my life with her. When you know, you know."

"Well as your first fake wife, I feel like I should give you my blessing. Lauren Ricci is a lucky woman to have won your heart Gage, especially since it belonged to me and Cordelia; she stole you from both of us."

"Iris," Cordelia looked towards her friend.

"She would have to be a special woman to do that, and she is." Iris raised her beer bottle in the air, "To Gage and Lauren, may they have a long and happy life together."

Everyone joined her in the cheers.

"I'm glad that the five of us can all be together like this again, I've missed it." Duke pulled Cordelia in closer to him.

"We've all missed it." James looked over to Iris and smiled.

"When's the last time we were all together?" Cordelia asked trying to remember exactly when it was.

"Up here, right before college. Cor, you left first for school, and then Duke and Gage left a couple of days later." Iris looked around at her friends, "That was eight years ago."

They all grew quiet.

"So much has changed in eight years, except for one thing, we're still friends." Cordelia looked around at the faces of the people she loved the most in the world.

"Gage, how does it feel to be the first one of us to get married?" Duke asked which caused James and Iris to both starts choking on their drinks, "What's going on with you two, are you okay?"

"Now or never?" James asked her.

"Now or never." She agreed as they looked at everyone. "Gage isn't the first one of us to get married."

Gage sat on the sand next to Duke and Cordelia as he tried to read Iris and James, "Who is?"

James took Iris's hand in his, "We are."

"What?" All three asked in unison before silence fell over them.

"The dream wedding you described, that's how you two did it, isn't it? No one knew, did they? Not even Samantha and Dennis?" Cordelia watched her friends face.

"Yeah, we've kind of had his on and off thing since college." Iris explained, "James pulled a total Harry on me on New Year's Eve this year.

You never come to the parties with me because you've been waiting for Duke on the roof."

"Why didn't you guys tell us?" Gage was shocked, he'd known something was going on with them, but he didn't know it was this involved.

"We don't know, we only told Dennis and Samantha yesterday." James looked away from his friends and towards the fire, "We didn't want you to look at us differently."

"We love you guys, and we want you to be happy. If you really do make each other happy, and it looks like you do, then I think we can all say you have our best wishes and blessings." Duke spoke as he kept Cordelia close to him.

"Okay, enough of this sappy stuff, let's get a picture of us all together," Iris suggested as they crowded around for a picture.

After the photo was snapped, Cordelia and Duke looked to Iris and both spoke, "You can hashtag that if you want."

"Really?"

"Yeah, I'm sure people will have lost interest if they haven't already," Duke told her.

@IrisLaArt
Last night where @CKNYC is single, oh and look whose snuggled together #CordukeReunion
@CKNYC
You know, this means after tomorrow Cordelia and Duke will be the only two of our group not married. @IrisLaArt @JamesSheath #CordukeReunion
@JamesSheath
Dude! @CKNYC Way to put us on blast!

CHAPTER 8

Something was nagging at Iris, keeping her awake, so she went and pulled up Cordelia's Facebook page and started to go through her pictures from various trips she took in college. She hadn't looked at them in ages, and never very closely since she felt left out. She also figured Cordelia obviously didn't look at hers either. They had led different lives then, waiting until the two friends could be reunited fulltime, and even now things were not what they had once been, but people change.

She thought all about the trips Cordelia had taken, thankful she set up an album for each of them. With each click, Iris's smile grew across her lips.

"James, wake up." She pushed his arm and he looked up at his wife with groggy eyes.

"Iris, how late is it?"

"Not that late, but I couldn't sleep and decided to go through Cordelia's college pictures on Facebook, look what I found."

James rubbed his eyes before taking the laptop and seeing in the background of a picture of Cordelia and her Sorority Sisters, none other than Duke, "Whoa, that's crazy, are there more?"

"Let's search, you get your laptop and look through Duke's photos."

James did as she requested and for the next hour, they spent it playing Where's Cordelia and Duke in each other's pictures.

"You realize neither of them noticed this, right?" James looked to Iris as he looked at a picture from the night Duke got his tattoo, "I mean look at this right here, they're in the same damn tattoo parlor, how did they not see each other?"

"No idea," Iris shook her head, "Part of me wants to tweet this out as evidence, but the other part of me is like they're already upset about that."

"Yeah, but I mean we could just tweet them to Gage . . ."

"I like the way you think Sheath." Iris pulled up twitter.

@IrisLaArt
Hey @GKNYC look what @JamesSheath and I found on FB #CordukeReunion

"I love you, you wicked woman you." James watched the way she smiled, every time he told her he loved it, it was like she couldn't believe it, even with their marriage.

"I love you to James, and I'm really glad we finally told everyone about us, getting married." She took his hand in hers, their fingers intertwining, "I am so happy to have you in my life."

"Well, I'm not going anywhere." He started to kiss her neck when someone started to knock on the door, "Who is it?"

"Gage, let me in."

James sighed, "If he wasn't getting married tomorrow, I would kill him right now."

Iris giggled, "Come in Gage."

"Hey, guys." He stopped as he took notice of exactly how the two of them were positioned, "I see I'm interrupting, I just wanted to know what made you look up these pictures."

"Curiosity, I mean come on Gage, they were so close to each other how many times? They're in the background of each other's pictures or they've just missed each other at places, look." She turned her laptop around to show him, "Like here in Tahoe, Cordelia and her Sorority Sisters were at this bar but left a little while before Duke and his Frat Brothers were there. It was like fate was teasing the hell out of them."

"Did you guys ever hope they would run into each other back then? We all knew they were going to the same areas for these trips, the same week."

James looked down, "To be honest, I was kind of hoping they wouldn't see each other. I knew how hurt Duke was, and how angry Cordelia was at least the first few trips. But then I just wanted them to run into each other and get it over with, but they kept missing each other. I think that's why none of us flat out told Cordelia that Duke was your Best Man. I think on some level, we needed nothing to stop them."

"I always wanted them to see each other, to just have it out like they probably did that first night here." Iris sighed as she tucked her feet under herself, "I'm just worried about what happens when she finds out that Duke is moving back."

"To be fair," James started, "We all thought he was going to stick around Texas, well except you Gage. But I think Cordelia needs to be comfortable with whatever rules they agreed to. I think she's trying to protect not only herself but him as well. You know in that weird way only Cordelia understands."

"I only knew he was moving back because we talked about it, and I brought him to see Beverly about the retail space." A smile crossed on Gage's lips.

"You schemed this, didn't you?" Iris's jaw dropped.

"I'm the wonk." Gage smiled, not sure Iris would understand, and he knew that James wouldn't get it. "Listen, Lauren and I are leaving for the honeymoon first thing Monday morning; I won't be here to help you pick up the pieces when he leaves."

Iris and James both sighed, knowing Gage had a special touch when it came to Cordelia, he always seemed to get through to her in ways that they couldn't.

"Maybe we won't have to." Iris was hopeful, "I mean she's preparing to live a life without him, right? I mean she's done that for the last eight years, so Monday night he's gone, maybe she cries it out because she misses him, or maybe she throws stuff around her apartment, or maybe she takes the dog for a walk around the city, I don't know but we have to let her feel whatever she's going to feel. We have to let her react however she's going to react unless she tries to hide it."

"I think it's best if we don't mention him to her, act like nothing happened this weekend," James suggested.

"Guys, we created a viral sensation over the two of them seeing each other for the first time in years. I'm not sure we can act like it didn't happen." Gage reminded them.

"How long is it going to take him to get his ass up from Texas?"

"Well if he has everything ready to go, say he gets loaded up Tuesday morning, he would arrive Wednesday night, unload Thursday morning, maybe." James thought about the drive, "But if he still has to pack, I don't know that could take a few days."

Iris nodded, "Let's hope that Duke is back in New York by Thursday, and after that, I don't know, he and Cordelia can have whatever damn timeline they need, or until I get sick of them not seeing each other."

"Oh, come on, he's moving into the same building she's in for work and business," Gage reminded them, "They'll have to see each other sooner or later, right?"

"Duke isn't stupid; the man is so crazy in love with her he might just knock on her door the moment he arrives." James thought for a moment, "Or he'll wait until Cordelia walks into his clinic with Scottie to get a chip put in."

"Anyone know when the clinic is supposed to open?"

Everyone shrugged.

"Were they always this exhausting?" Gage asked trying to remember.

"Always." Iris and James said in sync.

"Gage, we should all get some sleep. You have a big day tomorrow; think about how happy you'll be the life you'll be starting, not if Cordelia is going to be heartbroken from her own stupidity." Iris reminded him.

"Okay, night guys." Gage finally left.

James looked to Iris, taking her face in his hands, "I thought he would never leave, let's forget about Cordelia and Duke, worry about us, how does that sound?"

"Perfect, except one thing. I don't think we have anything to worry about." She kissed him, feeling the now familiar warm feeling that came over her every time his lips pressed against hers.

♥

"That's interesting." Cordelia had been scrolling through twitter on her phone, she almost never logged into it. She posted pictures to her Instagram, and then she would cross-post to Twitter and Facebook. She didn't even have her twitter notifications on, but her curiosity about if Iris, James, and Gage were still tweeting about her and Duke had gotten the best of her.

"What is?" Duke had been in the bathroom brushing his teeth and now stood in the doorway watching her.

"Apparently our friends decided to go through our old Facebook pictures." She clicked open the picture of her and her sisters from Mardi Gras, "They found something very interesting.'

"What?" He asked before gargling mouthwash.

Cordelia got up and handed her the phone to him, "Tell me where that picture was taken and when."

He took a look when he spat the mouthwash out and for a second he saw Cordelia and some girls he didn't know in matching pink shirts he recognized and he scanned the picture before spotting himself and several of his brothers in the background, "Is this for real?"

"They posted a few more." She scrolled to the next picture, "Look, Las Vegas, we went to the same tattoo parlor, the same night, it looks like we were there at the same time."

"How did we never see this before?"

Cordelia looked at her screen, "No idea, but they never noticed it either and they knew we were in the same places, that we both were going to Mardi Gras, or Tahoe, or Vegas."

"Maybe if they weren't looking for us in each other's pictures, they wouldn't have found us."

"It's silly now, of course, I want to pour over all my old pictures and see if I can spot you."

"You don't have to; I'm sure Iris and James have everything already found." He kissed her cheek as he came out of the bathroom and lay on her bed.

"You are awfully comfortable there, huh?" She put her phone on the charger and lay next to him, her head resting on his chest.

"I could say the same about you." He heard Scottie get up and jump on the bed, "Hmm, how do you feel about this?"

"Scottie on the bed, I don't know. I think I'm going to have to get him a bed of his own. You hear that boy?"

They could hear his tail wagging against the bedding.

"Oh, so he's staying with you?"

"Yes, he shouldn't have to go through the stress of flying." Cordelia rationalized.

"Good point." Duke kissed the top of her head, "What time do you have to be up?"

"Not until seven, I just have to check that the cake is still okay, and my baking duties are done until I go back to work on Tuesday morning."

Duke looked at the clock, "Then I get to hold you all night long, I don't plan on letting go."

"Good; because I don't want you to let go."

They turned off the lights except for a small one near the bathroom, pulled the blankets up and found a position that worked for them and Scottie who had already fallen asleep.

They didn't speak, they just enjoyed the comfort of being together and the silence, Duke played with her hair.

"Is *The Princess Bride* still one of your favorite movies?" Cordelia finally spoke.

A smile crept over his face, "Yes, it is. Why?"

"As you wish" She lifted her head to get lost in his green eyes and the moonlight.

"You caught onto that did ya?" He could feel the butterflies in his stomach.

"If you are using it to say, what I think you're trying to say—" She started just before the door of her bedroom opened and the lights flipped on.

"Cordelia, we need to talk." Tony froze when he saw his daughter in bed with Duke.

"Oh no." All three of them said at the same time.

"Dad, what do you want? It's after midnight." Cordelia refused to let her father's overprotectiveness get to her.

"Duke."

"I'm in your daughters . . . room?"

"Her bed!" Tony just stared at them, even though he'd given Duke his blessing it never occurred to him that things had progressed to this stage over the weekend.

"Dad, I'm an adult, Duke is an adult. We were just talking; we weren't doing anything else." Cordelia got out of the bed and went to guide her father out of the room, "What do you want?"

Tony looked at his daughter, and then at Duke, rationally he knew everything would be okay, "Are you sure you want to do whatever it is your doing with him?"

"Dad, I'm sure. Now go to bed, or I'm getting Mom to make you."

"Fine, fine" Tony left, and once Cordelia's door was closed, he heard the lock turn, he still wasn't ready to let go of his little girl.

Cordelia crawled back into bed with Duke, "Sorry about that, the one good thing about living in my own apartment is I can deadbolt him out, not that I need to, I don't have guys over in my bed."

"That's always good to know." Duke made a mental note to make sure he kept the deadbolt locked when he moved in, "So what were you saying?"

Cordelia shook her head, "It's not important."

"Cordelia, don't do that."

"Do what?"

"Get scared and back down." He took her hands in his and kissed each knuckle.

"Duke—"

"I love you, Cordelia Watson," He dropped her hands as his own raked into her hair, "I have since the day you fell into my lap on the subway, the first day of seventh grade. Every day since, even in this last eight years apart I have grown to love you more, deeper, stronger."

She bit her lip, "You have?"

"Of course, I have, why would I climb up that fire escape every year on Christmas Eve, hoping for the chance to see you, to talk to you, to figure out where we went wrong?"

Cordelia was silent, she closed her eyes, trying to fight back the tears in her eyes, "Do you know how many times I just wanted to hear your voice, to breathe in your scent, to feel your arms wrapped around my body again?"

"I have an idea." Duke sat up, taking her in his arms, "Don't cry Cordelia, we will figure this out."

"You're going back to Texas on Monday."

This was killing him, "Yes, I am."

"You've worked for this for so long, I couldn't ask you to change your plans."

"You're not, and you never have." He cupped her face in his hands, "Cordelia Watson, look at me."

She opened her eyes, the tears falling down her cheeks.

"I promise you; we are going to figure this out. I know you love me; I know you're afraid to say the words, but I already know."

"How can this work, I'm being a fool with my stupid one week a year idea." She felt her heart breaking as she realized she would never have the life with Duke that she had always secretly dreamed about.

"We will figure it out." He kissed her forehead, "Stay here, I'll be right back."

Cordelia didn't move as she tried to calm her breathing, stop her body from shaking, she looked up to see Duke come back with his wallet.

He sat next to her and smiled, "You remember the other night when you accused me of carrying around a condom in my wallet?"

She nodded as he handed the wallet to her, "Does that worn circle look like the size of a condom?"

"No." She confessed as she really looked at it, "What is it?"

Duke watched as she tried to wipe away her tears, "You see about eight years ago, the only woman I ever loved, ever could love, broke up with me over a goat."

Cordelia laughed because it really was funny, "That poor girl must be kicking herself over that."

Duke reached up, his thumb wiping away a tear, "We both are, but when she broke up with me, she sent me something that made me know she was serious about it being the end. When it arrived and I opened the package, I was devastated, and I shoved it into my wallet, where it has sat all this time."

"Duke?" She watched as the ring that had once known its place on her left hand appeared from the worn brown leather wallet.

"I gave you this with a promise that we would have a future." He picked up her left hand, "I'm making you another promise Cordelia, we do have a future together, someway, somehow."

She felt the familiar silver ring being slipped on her finger, and she realized now that she'd always felt that it was missing. "How can you be so sure, Duke?"

"Because I love you."

Cordelia looked into his peridot eyes, "I love you too Duke Shaw."

She felt his lips on hers and she believed him. They would find a way, it might not be easy at first, but they would figure it out, they had to. She had his promise ring back on after all.

He could've sworn he saw sparks of gold in her eyes when she told him she loved him. He was happy, and he knew he could keep his promise to her if she allowed him to.

They fell asleep in each other's arms, Scottie sleeping at their feet. This was their future, Duke knew it, and this was how things were always meant to be for them.

♥

Beverly had kicked Tony out of the bedroom when he wouldn't stop pacing, sending him down to the kitchen to get some warm milk and at least allow her to sleep. He hadn't expected to find Dennis sitting in the kitchen with a glass of his own.

"What are you doing up?" Dennis looked at his friend.

"I did something Denny, I had one last scheme in me, and I think it worked." Tony took the carton of milk out from the fridge, "Wait what are you doing up?"

"Iris is like my own daughter and I'm trying to figure out how to be okay with the fact that she and James—" He couldn't even finish the sentence.

"Dating, yeah we all suspected that for a while." Tony waved it off, "He's a good kid, great manners, though he would always finish the milk off."

"Married, they got married, Tony. How do I let my not so little girl go?"

Tony stopped and looked at his friend, "They what?"

Dennis nodded, "April seventh, they got married at the courthouse, didn't tell anyone except some of James's family in Texas."

"It's like a disease with these kids." He said as the microwave beeped with his milk. He went and sat down at the table.

"Wait, what scheme are you up to?"

"It was a long shot but getting Cordelia and Duke back together." Tony stirred the milk, "And it's working, I went in to talk to her and they were in bed together."

"Like in what way?" Dennis raised an eyebrow knowing his best friend had a way of making things sound worse.

"Clothed, in the dark, talking, that dog sleeping at the foot of the bed."

"You're upset that you tried to get your daughter back together with the only man she's ever loved, and it's working?"

"Yes." Tony took a sip of his milk, "I'm not ready to let her go, just like you're not ready to let Iris go."

"They're just talking Tony; you don't know that they're back together yet."

"He asked for my blessing again."

"Oh." Dennis nodded, "At least you got asked, Samantha and I got dragged into the library and told they've been secretly married for months."

Tony smiled, "Who would've ever thought that we would be sitting in Keller and Jennifer's beach house kitchen, late at night discussing our daughters together?"

"I think you saw that coming at some point, I don't think anyone else did." Dennis took a sip of his own drink, "Duke is a good guy right, he didn't cheat on Cordelia, right? He just had an idiot Frat Brother and Cordelia got scared."

"You read that NYCBuzz story huh?"

"How could I not, my daughter is the one tweeting about them—and her husband." Dennis shook his head, "Iris is married."

"Gage is getting married."

"Cordelia's back with Duke, this seems like a lot to process this weekend."

"Yeah, it does. So, let's not and just let them make a mess out of everything all on their own."

Dennis nodded, "Great idea buddy, wait who was in on this scheme with you?"

"Gage, he knew Duke wanted to move back, we just arranged so that he and Cordelia will run into each other when he gets back with his stuff."

"So that's whose moving in."

"Yeah, that's who."

"Still the king."

"Let's hope so."

♥

When Cordelia woke up, she knew it would be easy to get used to a schedule like that, not to mention waking up with Duke next to her. It could be perfect. When she saw the familiar silver ring back on her finger, she knew it could happen, somehow, someway, someday, and she could hold onto that for now.

Duke was still asleep next to her, soft snores from Scottie at the foot of the bed.

She left him and went to shower, knowing she had a lot to do over the next few hours before the ceremony and reception.

When she came out, her hair still slightly damp but clipped up she saw him getting Scottie ready for a walk, "So, you really carried this around with you every day for all this time?"

"I sure did, I knew one day I would give it back to you; that it would rest on your finger once more." He smiled at her, "Want to come with us, or do you have to go help the Bride?"

"Bride calls," Cordelia said just as her phone started to buzz and Lauren came up on her Caller ID.

"I guess I will see you at the wedding." Duke kissed her deeply before he pulled himself away.

"I'll be the girl in the red dress," Cordelia called to him as he and Scottie left.

She grabbed her make up bag, hairbrush and spray, and of course her shoes and dress before going down the long hallway to find Lauren getting ready.

Iris was already in there, still in her pajama's trying to get Lauren to eat something, but her nerves were preventing her from doing so. "Cor, any advice, you've dealt with far more Brides then I have."

"Small bites, one at a time." Cordelia handed her a piece of toast, "You love Gage, and he loves you. In your hearts you've already made a commitment for life, today you just verbalize it."

"Thank you, Cordelia." She took the toast from her and then grabbed her hand, "What's this?"

Cordelia dropped her head as Iris grabbed her hand from Lauren, "Is this what I think it is?"

"I don't know Iris, what do you think it is?"

The Bride and the Bridesmaid looked at each other, "The promise ring."

"Cor, I know this ring I helped him pick it out. It has stars engraved all around the band instead of stones." Iris couldn't believe what she was seeing, "What are you doing with this, how did you get this? Where did it come from, I thought you gave it back to him and that's how he always knew you were serious about breaking up."

"Slow down, Duke has apparently kept it in his wallet all this time." She smiled, but part of her wondered if she would've been open to wearing it again if they'd crossed paths earlier, "He gave it back to me last night after my Dad walked in on us."

"Wait, back it up." Lauren put a hand up, "Walked in on you doing what?"

"Yeah what did Watson see?"

"Nothing that scandalous; thank God. Duke and I were just lying in bed, talking and my Dad walked in. We were both in our pajamas, Duke didn't even run away."

"Cinnamon, that is enough to set your father nuclear."

"I reminded him that we're all adults and he left. I don't even know what he wanted to talk about."

"Okay, so how did you get this back?" Lauren took her hand again looking at the ring.

"We were talking, and Duke gave it to me, as a promise that we would be together again, that we didn't have to set anything in stone yet, but that we would figure it all out." Cordelia twisted the ring with her other hand, "I've felt like this has been missing from my hand for years."

"You will figure this all out; I know you will." Iris hugged her, "Now let's get this Bride all dolled up so Gage passes out in Duke's arms."

"What did you and James bet on that happening?"

Iris smiled, "A weekend away."

"By the way, tell your husband I am pissed that I didn't get to help pick out your engagement ring. Wait, Iris did he give you a ring?"

Iris lifted the chain she wore around her neck from under her shirt revealing a slim gold band and matching ruby ring, "I've been wearing them around my neck since the day after we got married."

"They're beautiful." Lauren told her, "I still don't get why this was all a secret."

"Yeah, why didn't you tell us?"

Iris shrugged, "I don't know, things between me and James have always been just between us. When he showed up at my loft on

New Year's Eve, I was so angry with him and then next thing I know he was telling me that he's loved me for years, started falling in love with me in high school."

"Aww," Cordelia sighed, "I never knew."

"I didn't either." Iris smiled, "I maybe had a little crush on him, but I could never act on it. And when I did, I pretended it was only physical."

"I'm happy for you, I'm happy for both of you." Cordelia told her friends, "Now let's get your hair done."

♥

"Okay Gage remember to breathe," Duke told his best friend as they finished getting ready.

"I'm going to try, but you'll catch me if I forget?" Gage gave him a hopeful smile.

"Of course, buddy."

"Great." Gage went over to his dresser, "I got you something, well more like I did something for you."

Duke wasn't sure he was going to like where this was going, "What did you do?"

"Well, I had all of your stuff brought up to New York the other day; it's in your apartment, waiting for you. Most of it should be unpacked for you, kitchen stuff, the television, all that. I thought it was silly for you to go back to Texas when you didn't have to and didn't want to."

"Gage, that's too much you really didn't have to do that."

"I have the means, the connections to do something like this for a friend. You've always done anything you could for me, and this is my way of repaying you." Gage smiled, "And James I didn't forget about you. I got you and Iris something, it was going to be a figure out your damn feelings present, but you guys did that on your own. Go on a real Honeymoon."

"Gage, you didn't have to do anything like that." James felt him slap the envelope in his hand.

"Enjoy it, and know if you hurt Iris, I will kill you, and Duke that goes for you and Cordelia, but I know you would never hurt her."

"We know." James and Duke responded.

"Okay, you ready?"

"As ready as can be."

♥

The photographer spent the morning taking pictures while people all over were setting up for the beachfront ceremony and reception. The ladies dressed and the guys avoided it for as long as possible, but now it was time.

"Are you ready?" Cordelia asked Lauren as they stood in the library, waiting for the signal before they would start on down to the beach.

"I believe so." She took a deep breath, "I never thought this would happen to me."

"Why?"

"Being different," She held the bouquet, "I wasn't sure anyone would ever accept it, but Gage did, and so did all of you."

"We love you just the way you are, especially Gage." Cordelia gave her friend a hug before helping to adjust the veil one last time before the music started.

Iris went out first in her blue dress, and then Cordelia followed, and finally, Lauren accompanied by her parents.

When Gage saw his Bride, he fell right into Duke' strong arms, who of course helped his friend steady himself before looking over to the Maid of Honor, causing her to blush.

The ceremony moved quickly, faster than Cordelia expected it would and before she knew it, she felt Duke guiding her up the aisle, while James guided Iris.

The pictures were a blur as they were all set up into different groupings, though by the end everyone was paired off in their own couples of course.

During the reception Cordelia grew nervous, she had never actually been present when one of her couples cut into the cake, sure she'd seen the pictures, they always sent her one, but this was different.

"You okay?" Duke asked as he placed her glass of wine in front of her at the table.

"Yes, thank you." She looked around, "This is so beautiful; I can still barely believe this is real."

"Very real," Duke took her left hand in his, his thumb rubbing over the promise ring, "Are you sure you're okay, you look nervous."

Cordelia looked down, "You still know me so well after all this time."

"I do, so spill." He told her before taking a sip of his pale ale.

"It's ridiculous Duke." She looked into his peridot eyes, "I've never actually been present when the couple cuts the cake."

"God, I love you." He told her before leaning in, kissing her softly.

"What was that for?"

"For being you Cordelia, I think it's sweet, and adorable that you're nervous for that. I get it."

"Thank you."

"You're welcome, Princess."

♥

Across the tent, Beverly felt Tony's hand on her arm, "He just kissed her."

"Why are you freaking out?" Beverly rolled her eyes, "You gave him your blessing for him to propose, not once but twice. What is wrong with you?"

"The rational part of me is okay with this, hell I set the whole thing up with Gage." He confessed, "But the other part of me wants to protect Cordelia from getting hurt again."

"Tony," Beverly made her husband look at her, "They broke up almost eight years ago because our daughter jumped to a conclusion. Duke Shaw has loved her since the day they met and vice versa. We should be thankful that Cordelia found that. Do I agree with him not telling her about moving back to New York, not really, but I also get it. This is their lives and we must let them live it. Besides they've kissed plenty of times before."

"You didn't see them in bed, laying there together." He let out a small protective growl.

"Tony," Beverly just shook her head, "They're going to get married one day, Duke is going to have a deadbolt on his door to keep you out, isn't he?"

"Maybe," Tony shrugged, "She looks happy though, doesn't she?"

"Beyond so," Beverly rested her head on his shoulder, "Not everyone can be us."

"True." Tony sighed, "So when do you think he proposes, the first time he sees her, or sometime after that?"

Beverly smiled, "Probably depends on how mad she is at first."

♥

"Good afternoon everyone, I'm Duke Shaw, the best man." He held up his champagne glass up as he looked around, "When I was in middle school, I moved here from Texas and made the best friends a guy could ever wish for. Gage, you were this goofy guy, but I couldn't help but be friends with you. You've done amazing things in this world, and I know that you and Lauren will continue to do so. Congratulations!"

Everyone cheered and clapped.

Cordelia rose, holding her glass tightly, "Hello everyone, I'm Cordelia Watson, one of Gage's fake ex-wives, the second one of course." She caught a look from Iris. "I've known Gage since pre-school, and he is one of the best friends a girl could ever hope for. Lauren came into our lives during middle school, and while we didn't always understand each other we were willing to learn. Seeing them together, now, so happy is what the world is all about; people change people, the secret of life. I love you both."

Everyone drank to the happy couple and Cordelia felt like she was about to cry.

"It's now time for Gage and Lauren to share their first dance." The MC announced as the band began to play the song they had chosen.

Cordelia held Duke' hand as they watched the newlyweds' dance, before trading off to dance with their respective parents.

"Gage and Lauren would like to invite everyone else to join them on the dance floor." The MC smiled as the couple swayed to their song.

"May I have this dance?" Duke rose from his seat, taking her hand.

"You may." Cordelia followed him to the dance floor, "How many dances have you gotten so far Dr. Shaw?"

"Not as many as I would like, but we have time, we also have almost eight years to make up for." He held her close, trying to figure out how to tell her he wasn't going back to Texas, that he'd only planned to do that so he could bring his stuff up, but Gage had it done for him.'

"Where do you want to go first?" Cordelia thought about all the trips they could plan.

"I like that South Dakota idea, go see Mount Rushmore, see a bit of the west. When do you want to go? When's a good time for you?"

"November, that's my slowest month at least cake wise, what about you?"

"I think November would be good." He spun her out before pulling her back against him.

"Do you think it will be cold?"

"Maybe, but not as cold as the winter."

They continued dancing, not only to the music, but around everything they both wanted to say, and neither would.

"It's now time for the Bride and Groom to cut the cake!"

Cordelia stood off as far away as she could, Duke was near her. "I've seen hundreds of pictures of this moment, but it means so much more than it's for them."

Iris had been snapping a few pictures throughout the day and couldn't help but get one of Cordelia and Duke while they'd been dancing. She didn't know what they were talking about, but both looked happier than she could ever remember seeing them.

@IrisLaArt

Look how in love these 2 crazy kids are; think they'll figure it out? Duke goes back to Texas tomorrow. #Boo #CordukeReunion

♥

"Cordelia, the cake is amazing." Paige their old school friend came over to tell her, "Will you be at the bakery this week? My parent's anniversary is in September and I would love if you could do the cake for the party."

"Of course, email me and we'll set up an appointment." Cordelia smiled.

"It's great to see you two together."

"Paige," Duke smiled, "Thanks for sending me the link to the article. I had no idea what anyone was talking about at first."

Paige thought for a second before her eyes went wide, "Oh yeah, wait you didn't know they were tweeting about you?"

"Nope, no idea."

Paige nodded, "Well, good luck. I'll see you in a few days, Cordelia."

"Look, everyone is enjoying the cake." Duke pointed out when Paige walked away.

Cordelia smiled, "Yeah, they really are."

"Cor, this is the best cake yet." Iris shoved a plate at her friend, "Duke, can I please borrow my best friend?"

"Sure."

Iris pulled Cordelia away from him, "Cinnamon."

"Yes Honey?" Cordelia asked as they started dancing to the pop song playing.

"Where should I make James take me for a weekend away; Poconos or Vermont?"

Cordelia thought for a moment, "Vermont I think, it'll be fall by the time you two can get away, and I bet the colors will be wonderful that time of year."

"Good idea." Iris looked around to James and Duke chatting, "So you and the Cowboy ever decide about the once a year thing?"

"I think I might take a trip in November to South Dakota, see Mount Rushmore, Crazy Horse, all that kind of stuff." She tried to dance around with her answer.

"You're not taking that trip alone I hope."

"No, I think I'll have someone with me." Cordelia looked towards Duke, "I know you think it's silly, but with where we are right now in life, I think it's a good way to keep things going."

"I still think you should ask him to come home to New York, but you know your relationship better than I do." Iris looked to James, "Can you believe James and I are married."

"No! You totally cut me out of being your maid of honor." Cordelia teased, "But I knew you two belonged together, and I'm happy you guys figured it out and one day, you'll tell me the entire story."

"I think you're taking it better than my Mom and Dennis."

Cordelia nodded, "You know, Dennis is a lot like my Dad, probably not ready to let you go. He might be your step-father, but he loves you like you were his own."

"Yeah, I think that was part of why we kept it secret."

"I'm glad it's out in the open." Cordelia giggled, "So are you changing your last name?"

"Not yet, at least not professionally. Maybe if we have kids. But before you get all excited to be Aunt Cordelia that is not happening yet we're not ready for a baby."

Cordelia smiled, "I'm gonna be Aunt Cordelia, one day."

Iris leaned in close knowing the song would change soon, "Ask Duke to stay."

"Iris . . . I can't."

"Trust me, you can."

Cordelia shook her head.

"Iris, may I cut in?" Duke asked as the song changed to a slow one.

Before Iris could answer James had taken her hand and whisked her away.

"Smooth move Shaw."

"Well, I figure I would have to steal whatever time with you I could." His heart raced as she put her arms around his neck, and they slow danced.

"When do you leave tomorrow?" She felt her heart tighten as she realized time was ticking away from them.

"The flight I booked isn't until seven," He started as he looked into her scared brown eyes. "but I canceled it earlier."

Cordelia stopped dancing, "Why?"

He took a deep breath, "What I needed to get back to in Texas, doesn't need my attention anymore."

She didn't understand, she just looked up into his green eyes, trying not to get lost, "How is that possible?"

"Well, what I had to do in Texas was pack all my stuff into a moving truck and drive a couple of days before getting to my new apartment."

"Oh no, did you lose the apartment?"

"No, I didn't." He sighed, trying to figure out how to say this. She was going to be mad. "Gage actually went behind my back and had all my stuff moved and mostly unpacked a couple of days ago."

Cordelia frowned, "Oh, I still don't get why you canceled your flight."

"Let's talk about this later, when it's just you and me, okay?"

She nodded, the happiness of the weekend fading away.

"Okay single ladies, you know what time it is!" The MC called out and Duke pushed Cordelia to join the group.

Cordelia felt silly as she stood to wait for someone desperate to catch it when it landed right in her waiting arms.

A few minutes later Duke caught the garter, Cordelia could see her mother holding her father back as they made their way through the silly tradition.

"At least I know I don't have to worry about Noah coming in and sweeping you off your feet when I'm not looking."

"No, you really don't. Noah was a lot of grand gestures, but he doesn't have my heart. He was never going to get it anyway. It's been yours since Iris threw me into your lap on the subway."

Duke dipped her, "Well remind me to thank her for that someday."

"And now we say goodbye to the happy couple, Gage and Lauren Keller! They will be off on their honeymoon in Australia, where they plan to take time studying the native insects." The MC's face cringed when he got to the last part, not what one would normally read.

Cordelia and Duke said goodbye to their friends "Just have fun; get lots of rest on the flight." She told him.

Gage smiled, "Be happy, no matter what happens tomorrow or next week, enjoy the life you have. You might find it's sweeter than you realize."

"What is that supposed to mean?"

Duke shot Gage a look, "I just mean that I think it's wonderful that the two of you have finally reconnected, I was about to make something happen if it hadn't been for the wedding. Enjoy the time you have together, I know this isn't the end for you, I have a feeling the two of you will figure this out."

"Have fun in Australia." Duke gave his old friend a hug.

"Yeah, you have fun setting up that clinic of yours; I can't wait to know more about it." Gage gave him a knowing smile.

Iris and James said their goodbyes as well, and eventually, everyone else had gone to enjoy the last few songs of the band, leaving the four friends alone together for the first time in days as they watched Gage and Lauren's limo lights vanish in the night.

"Duke, can I catch up with you later. I need some girl time with Iris." Cordelia grabbed her best friend by the arm. "I'm sure you and James have stuff to discuss."

"Of course, be safe ladies," Duke called out as the girls walked down to the beach.

♥

"Cordelia, what's going on?" Iris stopped her so she could take off her heels which were already filling with sand.

"We didn't get to spend as much time together on the beach as we had planned, so I wanted to take a walk with my best friend."

"You know Cor, I haven't seen you this happy in ages, hold onto that okay."

"I'm going to try." She stopped as the wind blew her curls into her face, "I was terrified of seeing him again you know. I think a part of me always knew he was coming to New York; I mean I should've. That he would see you guys, and you would all do what you all do best, try and protect me."

"We didn't want you hurt, and you never told us why you broke up with him. We just never brought him up on purpose." Iris sighed.

"Iris, he held onto this ring in his wallet for eight years, who does that?"

"A man so heartbroken and still so lovesick that he was never ready to let go." Iris shrugged, "I don't know, I've never had a guy love me that way."

"James is in love with you that way." Cordelia sat down in the sand, "Did he really run to you on New Year's Eve to declare his love for you?"

Iris sat next to her, "Yeah, we'd been fighting about everything and I told him I just didn't want to talk to him for a while. And there I was in my loft, surrounded by college and art friends, and James comes in, rushed up to me and kisses me. Tells me he's loved me for so long he doesn't even know when it started, and he can't live without me."

"I'm happy for you; I just wish I had known." Cordelia looked out towards the water, "I don't know what the future really holds for me and Duke, but I believe him. I think we will have one."

"Are you two doing that sappy goodbye thing tonight?"

"Actually, Duke is going to drive me and Scottie into the city tomorrow. Do you think you and James can find your way back without me?"

"Yeah, I think the husband and I can figure that out. When's his flight?"

"He said seven but mentioned that he canceled his booking, something about Gage going and setting up movers for him and unpacking his stuff in the new place. We got interrupted before he could finish explaining it."

Iris's eyes were wide, "Really, wow, so are you going to try and seduce him into staying in the city?"

"No, but I might invite him up and I don't expect him to turn me down if I'm honest."

"When you two get married please can I have a better color for my dress?"

"You look cute in this blue." Cordelia pouted, "And who says you get one, you eloped and kept the whole thing secret, maybe I'll just have Lauren as a bridesmaid."

"You wouldn't!"

Cordelia smiled, "True, but I don't expect to get married anytime soon."

"Says the girl who caught the bouquet." Iris laughed.

"You're going to be pregnant before I'm engaged."

"No way, I already told you, we're not ready for that."

Cordelia rubbed her hands together, "I think you'll get pregnant before I get engaged, let's make a bet."

Iris nodded her interest peaked, "Okay, it's got to be a good one then."

"If Duke and I get engaged before you find out you're pregnant, you get to pick our honeymoon destination. If you find out you're pregnant, before we get engaged, I get to pick the baby's middle name."

Iris thought for a second before taking her friend's hand, "Deal. Cor, do you ever wish things had gone differently between you and Duke?"

"Do I wish we had these last eight years together, yes and no, if I hadn't been a total moron and beyond insecure, I never would've discovered my love of baking, cake decorating. I wouldn't have made that amazing cake for Gage; I wouldn't own the bakery. I could never fathom wishing that away. I've grown a lot as a person in this time, just as Duke has. Maybe a higher power needed us apart from each other so we could become the people we are, the people we need to be."

"That is a wonderful way to look at it." Iris looked out to the ocean, "So, should I bring over ice cream tomorrow night or will you be okay?"

"Maybe on Tuesday night" Cordelia leaned her head on her friend's shoulder, "I've been kind of spoiled having so much time with him. I don' know how I'll last until we go to South Dakota."

"I have a feeling you won't have to wait too long to see him again. I think right now that the two of you have reunited, nothing is going to keep you apart, not even the space between Texas and New York."

"Thanks, Honey."

"No problem Cinnamon."

They sat in the sand, listening to the ocean a little while longer, enjoying their last night in Coral Shore before returning to the city.

♥

"Good boy Scottie," Duke told the dog as he and James walked in the opposite direction then the girls on the beach.

"What do you think the girls are talking about?"

"Us probably" Duke breathed in the air.

"So, your clinic will open on Saturday?"

"Yeah, I talked to Beverly, she said all my paperwork is ready, Steve told her that all the medical stuff arrived Friday, and Gage had movers bring all my stuff up and unpacked for the most part."

"You're not going back to Texas now, what are you going to tell Cordelia?"

He sighed, "No idea, I tried to tell her while we were dancing, but I just don't know how she's going to react. I'm scared James."

"Cordelia loves you; she wants to be with you. She might be angry at first but the minute she gets lost in your eyes it'll be forgiven." James looked to his friend, "Are you going to propose to her?"

"I have the ring; I don't want to scare her off right away though." Duke stopped to pet Scottie as they turned around. "What about you and Iris; you're married, children in the future?"

"Maybe, but not yet."

"Look at us James, two Texas boys who moved to New York and fell in love with best friends. How lucky are we?"

"Beyond lucky; especially you, you got dumped cause of a goat."

"You know, I'm not sure who has it worse, Cordelia for not realizing Wanda was a goat or me because it was part of my pledge."

"I think it's bad for both of you, but it's in the past and you can laugh about it."

"Scottie, ignore James. Listen, you are going to come with me and Cordelia to New York, you'll be staying in Cordelia's apartment, but I think pretty soon we'll figure out a way for all of us to be together in one apartment."

Scottie barked and jumped with excitement.

"I can't wait to see Cordelia's face when she realizes that you're back in New York for real."

"Neither can I." Duke had to confess to himself, he was pretty sure she'd get a bit heated at first, but he believed that she would eventually calm down.

CHAPTER 9

"I made a silly bet with Iris earlier." Cordelia and Duke were packing their things to prepare to leave in the morning. Both were their pajamas, finding a peaceful comfort in that.

Duke stood in the bathroom door, his toothbrush in his hand, "What did you bet?"

"Well," Cordelia pulled her hair away from her face into a ponytail, keeping it in place with elastic she'd had around her wrist, "She thinks since I caught the bouquet, that it automatically means you'll propose to me before she gets pregnant. So, I told her that if that were to happen, she gets to pick our honeymoon location, but if she gets pregnant first, I get to pick the baby's middle name."

Duke listened, and didn't speak as he brushed his teeth after he rinsed his mouth he looked over to Cordelia, "Where would Iris pick for us if you had to guess?"

"I don't know, Niagara Falls, it won't matter. I have a feeling she'll be pregnant soon."

"Cordelia, you didn't know they were even married, none of us did until yesterday."

"True, but I did know something was going on. It's just a feeling." Cordelia waved it off like it was no big deal.

Duke tried to hide the smile that crept on his face while he watched her. He still didn't know how to tell her. Suddenly he realized going back to Texas would be easier than telling her right now. "Say we did get married, I'm not proposing right now, where would you want to honeymoon?"

"Paris."

"I did pretty much promise we would be in Paris together one day." He smiled at the memory before kissing her, feeling her body relax under his.

This was everything that Cordelia had ever wanted. This was what she was going to have for the rest of her life, maybe not right away, but they would figure it out.

His hand slipped under her tank top, and she arched her body towards his, encouraging the touch. Cordelia shed her tank top and he lost his t-shirt before they began kissing again, nibbling necks and ears as fingers pushed away bottoms.

They were slow as they made love, each wanting it to last as long as possible. When she cried out his name, he couldn't hold back any longer. He held her afterward, neither moving, just listening to the heartbeat of the other.

They woke up at six, Scottie whimpering, in need of a walk.

They threw their pajama's back on; each grabbed their trusted hoodies and took Scottie for his last walk on the beach.

Over breakfast, Cordelia discovered her parents would be spending the week with the Keller' and Wagner's which surprised her, "Don't you have that new tenant moving into the retail space and building?" Cordelia was finishing her cup of coffee.

"Oh, all the paperwork is arranged, he has his keys, his stuff is even moved in already, he just needs to set everything up." Beverly looked to Duke over her coffee cup.

"Do you know when he'll be arriving?"

"Noon today I'm betting, maybe earlier. I wouldn't worry about it, sweetie." Beverly looked away from Duke and to her daughter. "Do you have any appointments set up for the week?"

"I have several cakes to do this week, and I know Paige is going to come on in for an appointment about her parent's wedding anniversary."

"So, you'll be busy, that's good." Tony looked up from his fruit salad, "I'm glad you're doing so well Cordelia."

"Thanks, Dad, but we should get ready to leave Duke; I know you wanted to get on the road soon."

"Yeah, we should. Mr. Keller thank you for letting us use your car, where would you like me to leave it.

Paul emailed Duke the address for his parking garage, "Just drop it off when you're done this afternoon."

"Again, thank you." Duke looked to everyone, "It was great seeing you all, hopefully, I'll see you all again soon."

Tony smiled as he watched his daughter and Duke leave.

"They're going to have a great honeymoon in a few months," Iris announced.

"Did Duke propose already?" Beverly leaned close to the young blonde.

"No, not yet, but she and I made a bet." She explained thankful that James wasn't in the room now, "She thinks I'll be pregnant before Duke proposes to her. I mean that boy is dying to pop the question."

"You know he asked for Tony's blessing again."

"Again?" Iris was shocked, "And he gave it to him?"

"They love each other, I will probably never be ready to let Cordelia go, but I see the way he looks at her, I hear the way he talks about her."

"Wow, well I hope he can afford to take her to Paris because that's my pick for them"

Beverly smiled, "Good choice."

"How mad do you think Cordelia is going to be at him when she finds out he's not going back to Texas?"

"I have no idea, I love Cordelia, and it's obvious to us that Duke is moving back to New York. But we're also not afraid of that next step. They've never been good about that. Part of why we're staying here, they're exhausting."

Iris giggled, "They really are. I tried to get her to ask Duke to move back, but she is dead set on him returning to Texas. How mad is she going to be at all of us?"

"Not as mad as she is at herself. I think at this point he could show her a picture of the building and she would say, 'Oh cool, you have the same style in Austin as we have.' She'll be thrilled when she realizes what it all means, but that hope, she's trying not to allow it to overwhelm her."

Iris nodded along; it made sense once she heard it out loud from Beverly.

♥

Cordelia was trying to find a radio station as Duke pulled out of the driveway; it seemed bittersweet to know that these were her last few hours with him, until November? She couldn't think about that; she couldn't think about the time they would spend apart.

"Aww, I love this song." Cordelia looked out the window Scottie was in the backseat, his head hanging out as they drove down the road.

"I remember when I first heard that song after our breakup." Duke began, "I was at a mixer, and it came on and this girl asked me to dance, I excused myself, because all I could think about was you, the last time we were together in New York on the roof of your building."

"The same roof we had our first real kiss."

"The same roof we decided to become boyfriend and girlfriend, officially."

"And the same one where we agreed to go to separate colleges." Cordelia was silent for a moment. "The same roof, I would wait for you on New Year's Eve each year. You might have been climbing fire escapes on Christmas Eve, but in my head, I always thought New Year's would be when you would show up."

"We were always so close, but so far at the same time, huh?"

"Yeah, I guess we were." Cordelia straightened up, insisting to herself not to dwell on the past, "Are you ever going to tell me the name of your clinic?"

"Okay, I guess I can tell you now." Duke felt the smile on his face, "Blue Dog Animal Clinic."

It only took her half a moment before she realized what he was doing, "Are you serious?"

"Yeah, I always thought it would be a cute name. I used one of the dogs you drew me ages ago for a logo, I hope you don't hate me."

"I have never hated you, Duke, I never could."

"Even when you thought I was dating a goat?"

"Even then"

"That's good to know."

"Why you plan on dating another goat?"

"Nope, Wanda is strictly my past, and you Cordelia Watson are my future."

♥

When they arrived on Cordelia's street, her stomach knotted, and she tried to keep from feeling the ache in her heart that was already growing.

When Duke opened the door for her, she hesitated to get out afraid of what life without Duke in it again would be like, especially now that she knew exactly how good it could be.

"Cordelia?" Duke held her tightly, "This isn't the last time you're going to see me; I promise you."

"What if something comes up and you can't go to South Dakota, or you don't come back for Christmas?"

"You will see me before then, I promise you." He kissed her cheek before going to get her bags. She slowly walked up to the front steps, digging through her purse for her key.

Duke plugged in the security code without thinking about it and Cordelia froze. How did he know the code, it got changed every few months?

"Did I tell you it already?" She couldn't remember if she'd told it to him.

He didn't answer as she walked down the hall to her apartment.

"I must've why else would you know it." She unlocked her door; the apartment was warm and stuffy, so she immediately went to open the windows.

Something was nagging at her though, why - couldn't she recall telling Duke the code?

Duke had come back in with Scottie and closed the door, "Are you okay Cordelia?"

"Yeah, I'm just not ready to say goodbye."

Duke pushed her hair behind her ear, "You don't have to say goodbye. Sit down."

Cordelia moved to her couch, a hand me down from her parents. "Duke, I don't want to talk right now. I just want us to share what time we have left."

"Cordelia—" How was he going to tell her? Before he could her lips were on his, white-hot heat emanating from her.

"We can always talk later." She breathed into his ear, "Right now, you're here with me and I plan on giving you a proper goodbye."

Her mouth found his again before could protest and they moved to her bedroom, stripping their clothes off as quickly as they could before falling into the bed, bodies becoming one.

Cordelia quickly fell asleep in his arms afterward.

Duke closed his eyes, wishing he could tell her. He climbed out of bed, knowing he had to go return the car.

He found a piece of paper and a pen.

Cordelia,

I love you more than I could ever put into words on paper. I will see you sooner than you think.

Duke

He left the note on the pillow, kissing her forehead before he left. He just hoped she wouldn't be furious with him when he showed up later.

♥

Duke was getting his bags out of the car when he found an envelope with his name on it. He knew that handwriting anywhere and everywhere. He pulled out the letter.

Duke,

I know I told you that I don't think I can ask you to move back to New York. Not after you've spent the past eight years without me building a life, building towards your own clinic. But I must ask. Come home, Duke. Come back to New York, you belong here with me and Scottie.

I know you won't move back to New York, at least not yet. Maybe in a few years once we've figured this all out, or maybe I'll move to Texas. We're still very young; we still have a lot of time before we must decide where to build our life together.

That's what I want Duke, I want us to have this amazing life together and I know we will. I can already picture it, us married in a small ceremony on the roof of my building at sunset on one of those last warm fall afternoons. I can see the Christmas tree by our fireplace, yes, we'll have one. Scottie will be laying near it, with our children playing nearby and the gentle snow falling outside.

Gage, Lauren, Iris, and James will all be with us during the holidays, all our children playing together, growing up to be the best of friends.

I waited eight years for us to be us again; I just hope I don't have to wait eight more for us to start our life together.

Come home to me Duke, come home to our future. I want to get started on it with you.

I've loved you for so long, I don't remember a time in my life when I didn't love you. Sometimes it hurts to love you, like when I pushed you and Iris together, or when I thought you were dating a beautiful blonde in college, even though you were supposed to be with me. I really do feel beyond ridiculous about Wanda the goat; I'm over the moon that you can forgive me. Duke Shaw, I will wait for you to come home to me, but whatever we have until then I will cherish. I never want you to not be a part of my life.

Love Always,

Cordelia

Duke fell more in love with Cordelia as he read the letter. He put his bags in his apartment, it was large, it had a fireplace, this was going to be their home he just knew it. But first he had to do a few things and he just hoped that she didn't spot him first.

♥

When Cordelia woke, she realized how late in the afternoon it was. She wasn't surprised to see the note from Duke, a part of her felt guilty for never letting him say what he needed to say. It was better this way. They would see each other again; she knew that now.

She took a quick shower before taking Scottie for a walk. Stopping to pick up some dog food for him and something for her own dinner. After they ate when they got home, she found her way to her parents' apartment. She needed to sit in the bay window, let its magic wash over her the way it did when she was younger. The moment she sat back on the cushioned seat she knows everything will be okay once again. She looked out at the city, finding comfort in the hustle and bustle around her.

Her phone rang, she checked the caller ID, realizing it wasn't as late as she expected it was. Shouldn't he be on a plane right now? "Hi."

"Hi."

"Hey." She felt the smile on her lips, somethings would never change. "I got your note."

"Good. Are you in your old room?" His eyes scrunched as he studied his own screen.

"Yeah, I felt like I needed its magic before I go to work." She studied the room behind him. "Where are you?"

"My new apartment remember Gage had everything set up for me. I'm about to hang up some of my artwork. I hope I don't disturb the neighbors." He smiled playfully.

"I'm sure they would understand."

"Do you have a lot of work at the bakery tonight?"

She shook her head, "No, not much. I just have to leave a list of what needs to be made for the morning and go through emails. I'm a little nervous about what I'm going to find."

"You should get some rest. Don't push yourself. You're on a normal person's sleep schedule, it might take you a few days to get back to your wacky Cordelia schedule."

"Haha cute" She playfully rolled her eyes.

"Yes, you are. One of the many reasons why I love you."

"I love you too." She didn't want to hang up yet, but she knew the call was ready to end.

"Get some sleep, cuddle up with Scottie. I'll be dreaming of you."

"I'll be dreaming of you too."

"Good night Princess."

"Good night Cowboy." She blew a kiss into the phone, watching him catch it before the screen went back.

Cordelia sat at the bay window for a few more minutes after the call ended. She did feel better; something was nagging at her though. How was Duke already in his new apartment? Even if he had gotten a flight while she was asleep, he wouldn't be back in Texas yet.

She rose to pace as she thought. Trying to put the pieces together. Sinking back into the bay window seat she sighed, maybe she'd fallen asleep earlier than she realized. Maybe her timeline for the day was just off.

Cordelia lost whatever train of thought she was having just as a car alarm went off outside. She could also hear Scottie barking at the intrusion.

♥

Duke could hear Scottie on the other side of the wall, sure the car alarm blaring outside was the cause. After a moment Scottie calmed down, the alarm had stopped. Duke had finally found his toolbox; Gage's people really had set up everything. Only personal items hadn't been put away.

He finally got the piece he wanted to hang up. Before he could start to hammer the nail, the buzzer went off. He quickly moved to the call box, "Hello?"

"Does the future Mrs. Shawn know you're here?" James laughed before grunting.

"Hi Iris, she does not." Duke shook his head before he hit the button to let them in. A moment later he opened his door to find his two friends, each with a bag of groceries.

"We thought you might need some help getting unpacked." Iris shoved the bag at Duke, "Wow, so much is done."

"Thanks to Gage," Duke told her just as he closed the door.

James set the bag he carried on the kitchen counter, "She thinks you're in Texas huh?"

"For now." Duke began unpacking the groceries, all the staples a person would need.

"Just go next door and tell her." Iris looked at his decorative fraternity paddle, "Really?"

"That's going in my office." He promised, "She'll find out when she's meant to."

"Just go next door and tell her." James encouraged.

"Why are you two so anxious? Dying to tweet?" his left eyebrow raised as he questioned them.

"Ouch." James felt the sting of his words, "But no. We just want you two to be happy."

"Don't you want every day you can with her? Why not have that time start now?" Iris crossed the kitchen space. "Go and get your girl, Shaw!"

"Stop meddling." His voice curt as something scratched at his front door, followed by a whimper.

James was the closest to the door, so he looked out the peephole to see Cordelia urging Scottie to the door. A chuckle escaped, "Scottie knows your nearby."

Duke went to the window that looked out on the street; Cordelia was walking Scottie towards the bakery. Breathing in the summer night city air, "Of course he does. Which is why I need you two to back off."

"Fine." They replied in unison, a soft smile on their lips.

"Thank you" Though Duke wasn't sure he believed either of them.

♥

Cordelia watched as she was sure she saw Iris and James leaving the building and going towards the subway. Scottie whined as they got in the building, rushing again towards the apartment that had just been rented out.

"Scottie" she sighed, picking him up, "Who do you think is in there?"

The dog began to bark towards the door, "Scottie, shh."

Cordelia carried him to her door, quickly unlocking it. Just as she closed the door, Scottie jumped from her arms and began whining at the wall shared by the two apartments.

It was now that she realized the dog thought Duke was on the other side, "As much as I wish he was there, he's not. It's someone else."

Scottie whined again as Cordelia urged him towards the bedroom. "Let's take a nap sweetie."

♥

When the alarm went off Scottie looked at Cordelia through his sleepy puppy eyes before quickly going back to sleep.

Cordelia shook her head, throwing the blanket off her body. She glanced at her phone seeing a text from Duke.

Good Morning Beautiful.

Cordelia bit her lip, quickly typing a reply, before going to take a shower. Once she was dressed, she woke Scottie with the word 'Walk', deciding he could spend the morning in the courtyard behind the bakery.

As she got him set up, she felt a chill in her body. Automatically she looked around, realizing a light was on in the apartment next to hers. She was thankful Scottie didn't know exactly where they were. Sure, that if he knew someone was up and about, he would start whining again.

Just after placing a water bowl down for Scottie she looked up to see a familiar form in the bedroom window. She had studied that body many times over the past week, the way it would walk across a room after a shower was bouncy compared to the way he moved around a kitchen. "That scoundrel!"

Scottie looked up, cocking his head with concern.

"You were right little guy. I was wrong. Now I just have to figure out my next move." Cordelia glanced at the window before going into the office.

Part of her was steaming mad, the other part of her was hurt.

She went and made herself a cup of coffee before waking her laptop up. Her email was bursting, she scanned each one, putting anything related to the tweets in its own folder. She attempted to sort out the important emails, find invoices to pay, the appointment for consultations. The way things were looking right now, she wouldn't be spending much time in the kitchen herself. She would be meeting with potential clients. Some found her from the tweets, others from the write-up for Gage and Lauren's wedding in the Times.

Once she was done with the first round of emails, she got up to stretch, she checked on Scottie who was content in the private courtyard.

She made a mental note to look up dog treats she could bake.

She got things started for the day, made a list of the extra tasting cakes they would need. The morning staff arrived, greeted by Scottie, each falling in love with him before setting on to start the day.

Cordelia watched as things came to life around her. The whir of the mixers, the heat of the ovens. The bakery had come to life for the day. She was lost in the early hustle and bustle of the day, even with most of it spent in the office, figuring out what appointments she could send and when.

♥

Duke had woken up early, part of him on Cordelia's wacky schedule, the other ready to get his clinic set up. He made a quick breakfast before going down to his new space.

He couldn't believe it as he looked around, this was really going to be his new office, his very own clinic.

As he worked through most of the morning, he started to see everything coming together. He was almost surprised. As lunchtime came he locked up, returning to his apartment to find a note on his door.

Hi;

Welcome to the building. Please forgive my dog for whining at the door. Here are some vouchers for the bakery next door. I'm sure you'll love the strawberry bread.

Your Neighbor,

Cordelia Watson

He looked at the note, then over to her door. Would she be home by now, or would she still be at work? He took a step towards the apartment door, his hand in a fist to knock, hovering for a moment before he stopped himself.

No.

It wasn't time yet, it just wasn't.

Duke retreated to his own apartment, wondering if he was making a mistake.

♥

Cordelia watched as Scottie whined towards the door. She went to check the peephole and saw Duke turning to leave. He'd lost whatever nerve he'd had.

Why didn't he want her to know he was here, right next door?

She sighed pulling out her laptop to get back to work through the emails, trying to wade through all the ones that had to do with just the tweets and people's opinions about if she and Duke should be together.

Why were people so invested? Sure, she could understand people they went to high school or college with, friends of theirs, but absolute strangers were emailing her.

It was as she got deeper into the emails, finding a few from people who actually also wanted to set up meetings for cake tastings, that she realized she hadn't read all the tweets. Duke had curated a few for her to read.

As she sipped her lemonade, she opened the actual story on NYC Buzz. She took a deep breath as she dug into the tweets her friends had started after a bottle of wine one night.

Warmth spread in her heart as she scrolled through the tweets. She could see how their friends just wanted them to be happy, they'd never intended to blow up their lives with attention. It had just been them expressing their own feelings, frustrations with each other.

Cordelia looked to Scottie who was still staring at the door. She closed the laptop as she got off the couch. She had spent eight years without him, why on earth was she going to spend another minute without him?

Scottie was right behind her as she opened the apartment door, stepping into the hallway just as she heard another door open.

Scottie's excited bark could be heard throughout the hall as the dog ran to Duke, jumping up and down.

"Hey, buddy." Duke attempted to pet the excited pup as he looked to Cordelia, "Hi Neighbor."

"Why didn't you tell me?" She instinctively wrapped her arms around herself.

Duke stepped towards her, "I was afraid that you wouldn't give me another chance, and before you protest, I didn't get one right away. Then you were so sure I was going back to Texas, that we could still be together, I thought if you knew I was going to be here, in New York, apparently right next door you would run away scared. I don't want you to run away from me, from us again Cordelia. I want us, I want this."

She hadn't realized he'd moved closer, closing the space between them until his hand was on her cheek and she automatically leaned into it. "I want us, I want this, I need you and me together Duke. I don't want one week a year with you, I want every day with you."

He sucked in his smile, breathing a sigh of relief, "I want that with you, Cordelia. I want every night with you, every day with you. I want the rest of my life with you."

She pulled him close, her lips taking his, needing his, needing him as they kissed. Confirming everything they had said in the physical action.

Relief swept through Duke as he held Cordelia close, feeling her body against his at this moment. It was everything he'd been too afraid to truly hope for.

"How did you know I was even here?" he asked when they pulled apart.

"Scottie kept getting riled up by your door, and then early this morning," her fingers played with the collar of his t-shirt, "I saw you from the courtyard in your bedroom. I recognized how you move around."

"Are you mad?"

Cordelia shook her head, her brown locks getting in her eyes, "I was confused at first, but I get it. No more secrets Duke, no more crazy ideas about having stolen time, and please no more goats."

"I promise, well unless I get a goat as a patient, but that's not that likely, this is New York City after all." He teased.

"Why were you leaving your apartment?"

"To come to see you, why were you leaving your apartment?" he raised an eyebrow.

"I decided I was done not having you in my life every day."

"Good. I'm not going anywhere Cor."

"I don't plan on going anywhere either." She slipped her fingers with his, "By the way, were Iris and James at your place last night?"

"Yeah, how did you know?"

She shook her head, "I saw them leaving. That should've been a clue it was you next door."

"I'm glad it happened like this, it's our moment, not theirs."

Cordelia kissed him again, "Any plans this afternoon Dr. Shaw?"

Duke lifted her in his arms, carrying her towards his apartment, "Just showing you my new apartment."

She giggled as he carried her in through the door, it felt right, it felt honest, it felt real, all because it was as Scottie followed them in. He found a spot he liked just as Duke kicked the door shut before carrying Cordelia to his bedroom.

EPILOGUE

Cordelia took a deep breath, trying to remind herself to count to ten. She had nothing to be nervous about. Looking at her reflection she almost couldn't believe it.

"Are you ready sweetheart?" Tony stood at the door of her old bedroom, a smile on his face.

"I am I've waited a very long time for this."

The roof was decorated with white lights and flowers. A small band played in a corner as everyone gathered for the ceremony.

Duke waited, his heart racing with Gage and James at his side. Lauren and Iris had both walked down the aisle wearing deep purple dresses.

The music swelled, and Tony escorted Cordelia down the aisle. It was finally happening; he was going to have to let her go.

The moment Duke saw her; he knew this was one of those moments he would remember forever. He could barely breathe as he watched her, in fact, he was sure he would fall over and Gage and James would both have to catch him.

"Friends, family," The minister began, "We are gathered here this evening, to unite Cordelia and Duke in matrimony. Who gives this woman to this man?"

"I do, I know she'll be in good hands." Tony kissed his daughter's cheek and placed her hand in Duke' it was true, he knew that Duke would do anything for Cordelia; he would take care of her.

"Duke and Cordelia have written their own vows, Duke?"

"When I first moved to New York, I was starting over, I had no idea what to expect, I wasn't sure I would make friends. My first day of school, you fell into my lap on the subway; I knew then that I had to get to know you. You became one of my best friends, the only woman I have ever loved, even when we were apart, my heart was filled with love for you. I promise you Cordelia; it will always be filled with love for you."

"Cordelia"

"That day Iris pushed me into your lap changed my life. I knew you would be important to me Duke, always. I might have been scared and insecure a few times, but that's over. You always had my heart; you were always the man for me. My future has always included you, even when I couldn't see it. I promise you that Duke."

"These rings are a symbol of your undying love, and the commitment that you are verbalizing now, in front of friends, family, and God. Duke repeat after me, with this ring, I thee wed."

Duke smiled as he slipped the gold band on Cordelia's finger, "With this ring, I thee wed."

Cordelia bit her lip as she took Duke hand and slipped the band on his finger, "With this ring, I thee wed."

"By the power invested in me by the State of New York, I pronounce you Husband and Wife. May I introduce to you for the first time, Duke and Cordelia Shaw." He looked at the happy couple, "You may kiss now."

Duke cupped her face in his hands kissing her, a magic moment between just the two of them.

♥

"Are you ready to finally be in Paris together?" Duke held her close as they shared their first dance.

Cordelia smiled, "I almost can't believe it."

"Well believe it, tomorrow by this time we'll be in Paris."

He spun her out, pulling her close to him. "Dancing with you is one of my favorite things."

"Mine too, though it's a little weird having so many people watching us." She confessed.

"Let me guess, you prefer our moments in the kitchen?"

"How could I not?" She kissed him softly, quickly.

"We have a lifetime to dance in the kitchen together."

Cordelia giggled as he dipped her, "Duke Shaw, you charming devil."

"Only for you, Cordelia Shaw."

"Oh, I like that." She smiled.

"Okay, they're finally married. Think they'll be less exhausting?" James looked to his wife as he bottle-fed their son.

Iris snorted, "These two? Never, but we love them no matter what."

They watched their best friends dance. "She did pick a good middle name."

"Yeah, she really did, didn't she Dennis Wagner Sheath?" Iris kissed her son's forehead. "Do you know where he's taking her on their honeymoon?"

"Paris, like he's always wanted."

"God they're sappy."

"Well Tony, you did it. You let her go." Beverly took her husband's hand, "She'll always be our little girl no matter what."

"I know, if it had been anyone else, I don't think I could've done it. I knew this was how the story would always go."

"So, Husband, what happens next?" Cordelia was amazed at how she could still get lost in his eyes for even the smallest moment.

"Besides the dream honeymoon," He raised an eyebrow, "We could start thinking about what should go in that spare bedroom."

"Oh, I already know what that's going to be, we'll paint it a nice creamy, buttery yellow." She told him, a secretive smile on her face.

"Oh really, why yellow?"

"It's good for a boy or a girl." She teased.

"Cordelia . . ."

"We're not yet, but I think we're ready to start trying."

"I love you." He kissed her, deeply, slowly.

"So, are we going to make a bet on when we get a Corduke baby?" Gage sat with James and Iris.

Iris watched the couple dancing, "Oh, I say about nine months from now, give or take a week or two."

"You think honeymoon baby?" Gage looked over at them, "Yeah probably."

Iris pulled out her phone and took a picture, a smile on her face.

@IrisLaArt
So happy for my best friend, my sister, Cordelia today. #CordukeWedding

ABOUT THE AUTHOR

Kat Halstead lives in Colorado where she spends a good chunk of her time as the co-host of A Very Special Podcast, Getting Catty with Kat & Pat, and a few other shows. She is currently working in the real world, hanging out with her adorable nephew, and daydreaming about Chris Evans. You can find out more at kathalstead.net or by following her on twitter @katdvs.

52530564R00158

Made in the USA
Lexington, KY
16 September 2019